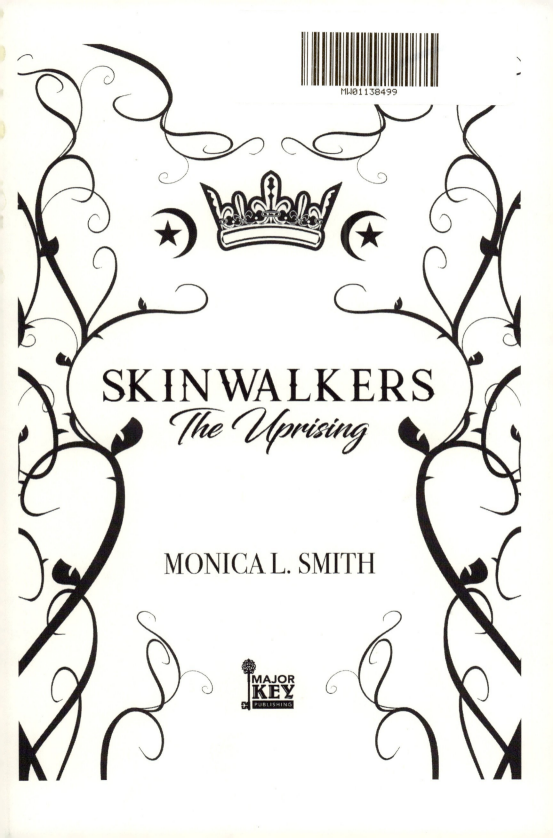

SKINWALKERS
The Uprising

MONICA L. SMITH

MAJOR
KEY
PUBLISHING

Sent with love and dipped in chocolate kisses, Enjoy, Monica L Smith

I would like to dedicate this book to the ladies who gave me the idea of writing a book about Skinwalkers. Although I have changed a lot of it to suit the needs of this story, it was because of Ashley, Sharon, and Micah that I created this book.

I gained a lot of knowledge from each one of you and have even borrowed your names. From the deepest depths of my heart to its surface, I want to thank you for all your support, input, and guidance.

CONTENTS

I have so much rage running through my veins. How could you love someone so much and hate them at the same fucking time? I gave my soon-to-be ex-husband the world, and in return, he politely showed me his ass to kiss. I wish he would drop dead somewhere, or at least have a heart attack or something.

When I met William, he worked for a fast-food restaurant as a damn cook. I was caught off guard by his flirtatious personality and dazzling good looks. I have always been a fool for a tall, dark-skinned brother with a big ass bulge in his pants. But I was the one who got the wool pulled over her eyes. I inadvertently allowed that son-of-a-bitch to hoodwink me. Once he became somebody, earned a little money thanks to my real estate company that I gave him a position as a manager in, and I dressed him in nothing less than the best; he dumped me and put another woman on his arm.

Now, while he is outliving the high life, I am sitting here in my bedroom drowning my sorrows in a cheap bottle of vodka. This shit is so cheap that it doesn't even have a name, and it burns the hell out of my throat when I'm swallowing it. But when you want some southern comfort to ease your pain, you need to downgrade to the cheapest shit possible. It gets you drunk so much quicker than the good stuff. Yeah, I'm going to have one heck of a headache and possibly be sick from a hangover – but it's worth every gulp I take. I love the way it numbs my pain.

Although the vodka helps, I can't help but think about what he has done to me and is now doing for her. I was pregnant at the same time she was. Need I say that we were both pregnant by the same man? While I was lying in a sterile room, on a hard bed, having a miscarriage with our child, he was out buying his whore a push present. With the money from our joint account, he purchased a Lexus for his new fiancé. Then, the day he served me with divorce papers, he withdrew fifteen thousand dollars and paid for her engagement ring. And even after all that, my stupid ass still wanted him here with me. But this will all be over in the morning because my divorce will be final.

As I finished a fifth of vodka, I continued to read this book that I had picked up earlier, *'Wicca, Protection & Hexes.'* I have never played with black or white magic before, but if it could bring me some peace and tranquility into my life and cause harm and destruction in his, I was all for giving it a whirl.

I found a couple of spells that I wanted to try. One was a protection spell to keep the dark spirits from attacking me while casting my spell. Another was a curse that would increase his fiancé Laura's sex drive while decreasing William's, making him impotent. But with the hatred overshadowing my better judgment, I need to go a step further. So, I read a little farther down and found out with a simple hammer and nail, I could also inflict a horrible sickness on him.

I was feeling extremely good and in the mood to cause havoc in his life. I wanted to cause as much heartache as I could to show him exactly how it feels when someone you love rips your heart right out of your chest and stomps the blood out of it. BASTARD!

I stumbled over to my window, grabbing for anything in sight to brace myself from falling, just to verify the moon was still full. Yeah – I know that was stupid, but it was important for this so-called spell to work. My vision was blurry, but the moon was so big and bright that it was impossible not to see it. But it wasn't the gorgeous ivory color like most nights; it was a lava red with butterscotch yellow and apricot orange hints scattered within it. The moon wasn't only full, but it was what one would call a blood moon.

After standing there for a while, taking in the beautiful sight of the moon, I turned away from it and tried to steady myself. I needed to pull myself together so I could move around the house to gather my supplies. I gave the room a chance to slow down because not only was it spinning like a tornado, but with every step I took, I felt as if the ground was shaking beneath my feet.

According to the spell, I needed a picture of William, Laura, four black candles, some cayenne pepper, salt, a few leaves from a Saw Palmetto bush, one nail, and a hammer. With my book clutched under my arm like a purse, I stumbled into the library. I had a few pictures of William and his lover on my desk, provided to me by the private investigator I hired. As I pulled their photos from the envelope, rage ran rampant throughout my body like a cheetah running to catch its prey. "You are a sorry ass son-of-a-bitch!" I yelled aloud.

With tears streaming down my face, I made my way to the kitchen. Luckily, I had some black candles from a Halloween party we hosted a couple of years back. I laid the book on the table and began searching for the additional items needed.

Holding onto the counter, I yanked the drawer open, sending it flying across the room. Since I was too drunk to walk across the room and bend over to pick up the candles, I took the easier route and crawled over to them on my hands and knees. As I crawled on the floor like a three-year-old, I thought to myself, *'A drunk ain't shit.'*

I grabbed the candles and made my way to the table, and pulled myself up onto my feet. I managed to make it to the spice cabinet to retrieve the cayenne pepper and box of salt. I stumbled out to the garage, found William's toolbox, the hammer, and a nail. I opened the garage door and made my way to one of the many Saw Palmetto bushes surrounding my house. What are the odds that this plant is native to Florida?

I slowly picked a couple of leaves from it, made my way back into my garage, and hit the button to close the door. As I made my way back to the kitchen, I bumped into every wall I encountered and broke the heel off one of my Saint Laurent Opyum sandals. I didn't care, though; I just took them off and tossed them across the room.

To cast my spell, I had to protect myself from the dark spirits that would enter my home. I know that this sounds like a bunch of bullshit, but no harm, no foul.

I picked up the salt and began to walk around my kitchen, pouring it along the baseboards. I had to make sure that there weren't any breaks in the line. And as I made my rotation around the kitchen, I had to say the Lord's Prayer. With my words slurring and as I placed the salt on the floor, I recited it:

Our Father, who art in heaven,
Hallowed be thy Name,
Thy kingdom come,
Thy will be done,
On Earth, as it is in Heaven.
Give us this day our daily bread.
And forgive us our trespasses,
As we forgive those
Who trespass against us.
And lead us not into temptation,
But deliver us from evil.
For thine is the kingdom,
And the power, and the glory,
Forever and ever.
Amen.

As I finished the prayer and closed the circle of salt around the room, I felt a surge of serenity wash through me.

Now, to be fair, I cannot say for sure it was the protection spell or my drunk imagination that was playing tricks on me. But whatever it was, I thoroughly enjoyed the peaceful feeling that engulfed my being.

I stumbled back to the kitchen island to search the drawers for a lighter. The gods must have been smiling down onto me because it was in the first drawer that I gently pulled open. I grabbed it and made my way over to the kitchen table.

Holding tightly onto the kitchen table's rim, I walked to each corner and placed a candle on its edge. I lit them after I placed them down. When I had them all in place and lit, I picked up Laura's picture, placed it on the east side of the table, and sprinkled it with the cayenne pepper. Then I picked up William's picture, put it on the table's west side, and sprinkled the Saw Palmetto leaves onto it. Then I raised my arms to the Heavens and yelled a prayer to the Archangel Samael:

Finally, be strong in Him and His mighty power.

Put on the whole armor of Him so that I can take my stance of revenge.

For my struggle is not that of the flesh or blood, but the matters of the heart.

Bless me with your guidance, attention, and divine intervention.

Grant my request and repay the heartache that William and Laura gave unto me.

I could feel the air warm, causing me to sweat profusely. The flames on the candles grew larger and burned redder. And the pictures began to fold inward, catching fire at their corners. I picked up the nail, placed it into the middle of William's picture, and hammered it into the table. How I was able to hit the nail was beyond me.

As I hit the nail with my final blow, a calm wind blew into the room and blew out the candles. So, then there was blackness.

Dream:

It was a cool morning, and I was walking through a field of lilies. But as I looked at myself, I wasn't the flawless woman I knew. I had blue eyes and beautiful white hair. Instead of walking upright, I paraded around the field on four feet.

I was being followed by many who looked like me, who worshiped me, who loved me. Being around them, I was overwhelmed with the feeling of acceptance and belonging. They looked to me for support, guidance, and direction.

Although I was overwhelmed with the sound feeling of being surrounded by family, I wasn't born into this world as they were. I was gifted this life through a long line of heredity where they had to work for their blessing.

Together, we were running as one. I was free. My senses were heightened; I could hear the whispers of the night, smell the intimacy in the air, and feel the serenity that surrounded my essence.

I could breathe, there was no stress, and somewhere close – I could feel the love I shared with the other half of my heart.

Then I shifted back into my human form. This time I was in spirit, looking down onto my followers. But my followers weren't the same as those who ran beside me in the field of lilies.

These people were lost, confused, and alone. They were looking at me for answers, but I had none to give them. They wanted me to choose a side, but I wanted to be in both places.

My happiness was stolen from me, and I was crying now.

"WAKE UP!" I heard a thunderous voice yell.

I opened my eyes and realized that I must have passed out after drinking a whole bottle of vodka. The sun was blinding me, and as I began to stand up, I noticed that I was lying in a puddle of urine and feces. When I stood up entirely, although I was a hot mess, I laughed at that stupid ritual that I attempted to perform. As if that shit really works.

Disgusted with my soiled clothing that hugged every inch of my body, I stripped and tossed them into the garbage. I tried to clean up all the mess on the floor as best as possible, but I wasn't really concerned about it because the house had been sold, and they had to come and clean it anyway.

I hurried upstairs to jump directly into the shower. I needed to get that horrifying smell off my body. Before jumping in to wash away my sins, I turned on the television to see what was going on in the world. I couldn't live without my CNN morning news. But as the date displayed across the screen, I became immediately confused. I had lost four whole days. I must have hit my head and was knocked unconscious when I blacked out the other night. And the fucked-up thing about this situation is, I could have been dead in here, and no one would have ever known until they were due to come to the house to move my furniture out.

Now, I have to rush while trying to get over this ill-feeling about what happened to me a couple of nights ago. Because today is July the seventeenth, and it is seven o'clock in the motherfucking morning. I had exactly two hours to pull my ass together and get over to the Duvall County Courthouse.

Usually, it wouldn't be a problem for me because I am a diva by God's design. To me, a woman should wake up every morning and put on her best face, even if she has been dealing with her demons. I was taught at an early age that what you do to get him, you need to continue to do after the marriage to keep him. But due to the circumstances, I was going to try and pull off a miracle this time.

I thrive on making my presence known as I command attention when I enter a room. I was not only beautiful and intelligent, but I was a boss to all who knew me. When I opened my mouth, my words were calculated, precise, and stated their true intentions. You could never say that you didn't understand the words that fell elegantly from these luscious lips unless you were deaf. But even then, my body language spoke volumes.

Besides, I couldn't allow William to see how he was ripping my soul from my body. So, although I wasn't in the right state of mind, I took a quick shower and dressed in a cute white blouse that hugged my breasts perfectly, a pair of high-waisted black slacks, and a pair of six-inch heels. One thing about me, although I'm stressed, you will never see me sweat.

After perfecting my bitch face, I hurried to my sixty-five Shelby GT and sped downtown to the courthouse. I rushed up the steps of city hall, trying desperately not to be late for court. It didn't help that I had a pounding headache and that my eyes were sensitive to the glistening sun. The judge was finalizing my divorce today, and I had to mentally prepare myself for whatever may happen.

The closer I got to the courtroom, the more pissed I became. All I could do was think about his inconsiderate, ignorant, good-for-nothing, money-hungry ass and how he cheated. And for all my family and friends that knew what he was doing, they could kiss my ass too. Everyone knew that he was sleeping with another woman, but those sorry bitches didn't say one word. All of them were smiling in my face while laughing at me behind my back. But we will see who will get the last laugh. After this divorce is final, I'm taking the first flight out of this ghetto ass place and returning home, to where my roots were grounded. But not before they all find out that as of the day my divorce is finalized, they all will be unemployed. I had sold the business and put it in the contract that everyone related to me was to be fired, and none of them were to be re-hired under the new owners. Besides, I stayed on board with the new owners as the CEO, and I just couldn't have people under me that I didn't trust.

And poor William was going to get what he deserved. I was laughing on the inside, knowing that he would be left with nothing. He came into this marriage broke and willingly signed a prenup. So, he wasn't entitled to anything. Shit, my badass was cumming revenge. The only thing I was willing to give him was the bed he shared with me but invited his whore into. That – he could have.

I made my way inside the building and to the elevator. I pushed the up button once, twice, maybe even three or four times – who fucking cares? Then I heard someone say, "You only have to press it once. Trust me; it's coming."

I looked around with pure disgust in my eyes and noticed the police officer standing beside me. "What?" I asked him with a frustrated tone.

"The button. I see that you just keep hitting it. That is not going to make it come down the shaft any sooner," he chuckled.

If looks could kill, he would be dead. I stared at him, and it wasn't because I thought he was attractive or anything, but I wanted to ask him a serious question – from a man's point of view.

"Who leaves a young, attractive, financially independent woman for an easy piece of ass?" I knew the question was irrelevant to what he was saying, but it was on my mind.

"I'm sorry. Did I miss something here?" he asked, confused by my question.

"Never mind," I replied. "I knew better than to ask a man that question anyway. I don't want you to break your bro' code," I snapped, stepping into the elevator. He was looking at me, mortified by my answer as I gently pressed the number three. So, I felt the need to explain myself and said, "I only pushed the button once this time. Happy now?" He continued to gawk at me as the doors closed. As I stated earlier, it was impossible to misunderstand the words that fell elegantly from these luscious lips.

As I stepped off the elevator, I heard two people yelling at the end of the hallway. I listened to a woman screaming, "Who are you fucking that you haven't been able to get it up for me? You limp dick bitch!"

"Lower your fucking voice!" I heard him try to hush her.

As I took a couple more steps toward the courtroom, I heard her yell again, saying, "You either tell me who the fuck she is, or I'm going to give Ashley some dirt on your ass that will win her this entire case. Fuck with me if you want to, William."

"Laura," I smiled. "Problems in the relationship already?"

"He's probably fucking you," she snapped.

"No. No. No. That ship sailed a long time ago. He's all yours," I laughed, leaving them to continue their argument in the hallway.

I was ready to call it quits and get this divorce finalized. I had my fun running William's ass into the ground by making him go to couple's therapy, having him move out of the house because *I feared for my life*, plus I had his name removed from all the accounts and credit cards. Then to add some sweet icing to the cake – I fired him. He had to go out into the real world and find a job on his own. *The nerve of me*, I giggled to myself. I was so good at being so evil. Yeah, I had to pay him spousal support while this divorce was in progress, and I may have to pay him for a couple of months afterward, but it made my pussy tingle with excitement, knowing that I was getting under his skin.

I walked into the courtroom with my head held high. I looked sharp as a tack and as wise as a librarian – I was ready for action. My body is tight and firm, my outfit was expensive but professional, and my hair, make-up, and nails were all fucking flawless. There was no way in hell that I would allow him to see that he had broken me, that he had destroyed my very being.

William and Laura walked in behind me, still fussing about his limp dick issues and her overactive sex drive. If I really believed in the voodoo shit, I would pat myself on the back for all the misery and mischief I had added to their lives.

"Please, rise," I heard the officer say as the judge walked into the room. After she made her way to the bench and took her seat, the officer then stated, "Please, be seated."

I sat beside my attorney, placed my arms on the table, and smiled. I had a feeling that I was going to come out of this courtroom victorious.

My attorney leaned over to me and asked, "Is there anything else you want to ask for? This is the last day for any adjustments."

"Yeah. As a matter-of-fact, there is," I replied. "I want the judge to grant me my maiden name back. I want to be known as Notah again." I wanted to be separated entirely from William; besides, my great-grandmother was from the Navajo tribe, and I wanted to return to my roots. Not to mention, I plan to move back to Winslow, Arizona, where I had inherited plenty of land. During this ugly divorce, I visited a couple of times while my home was being built. While there, all the stress of this horrifying divorce was melted away by the Arizona sun.

"Today, we will be dissolving the marriage between William and Ashley Legend. Have we reached a final agreement?" the judge asked, fumbling through the stack of papers in front of her.

"No, Your Honor. Mr. Legend requests that his spousal support continues for the next twelve months, giving him time to find suitable employment. He is also asking for Mrs. Legend to continue to make his car payment and pay off a home loan that he acquired while still married to Mrs. Legend. We were originally asking that the home they shared while married be given to Mr. Legend, but we have recently found out that the home has been sold."

The judge looked through the papers again and then at my attorney. "Is your client in agreement with these new requests?" she asked.

"No, Your Honor. Since the first court date, which was well over a year ago, my client has given Mr. Legend fifteen hundred a month. She also offered him the Honda Civic, which he refused to take because he wanted to keep the Lexus he purchased for his new fiancé, Laura Jennings. So, therefore he should be responsible for the car payment, not my client. Lastly, Mrs. Legend shouldn't have to pay for a home for her soon-to-be-ex-husband to share with Mrs. Jennings. As for the home that was sold, that home was deeded to Mrs. Legend's mother, who is currently in an assisted living facility. The money gained from the sale of that house will pay for her mother's care while residing there."

Now the judge was cutting her eyes in William's direction. "Is this true? Mr. Legend is already cohabiting with his fiancé and wants Mrs. Legend to pay for the home?

"No, Your Honor. Mrs. Jennings does come over to the home and stays a couple of nights, but she does not currently live in the home with Mr. Legend," his lawyer stated.

"Really?' she asked sarcastically, sucking her tongue between her teeth. "Tell those lies to someone who cares," she snapped.

As she continued to rifle through all the paperwork, I whispered into my attorney's ear. She nodded her head and then said, "Your Honor, my client is also requesting that her maiden name be returned to her. She wants to officially cut all ties to Mr. Legend."

The judge looked at William with disappointment in her eyes before granting my final request. I could tell that he wasn't her favorite person, especially when she noticed his fiancé sitting behind him with a massive smirk on her face.

"So, let it be ordered on this day, July seventeenth, two thousand eighteen, that William Legend and Ashley Legend have not been able to resolve their marital differences. This court hereby orders that Mrs. Legend will pay spousal support in the amount of two thousand dollars a month for the next six months. This should be enough money for Mr. Legend to pay his mortgage or car payment. After the first day of the sixth month, the spousal support will cease, and Mr. Legend will be responsible for paying all bills independently. All other accounts and properties will remain with Mrs. Legend because all those items were obtained before the marriage or inherited from Mrs. Legend's father. Also, let it be placed on record that Mrs. Legend is entitled to obtain her maiden name of Notah," the judge announced, slamming her gavel on top of the small wooden circle.

The judge got up from her seat and walked out of the courtroom. I sat there for a few minutes, trying to hold myself together. My marriage to William was officially over.

I allowed the happy couple to leave the courtroom together before getting up and leaving. As I walked out of the doors, I heard William and Laura in another intense argument. She was still complaining about him not being able to get his dick up, and he was yelling back at her, saying she had become a nymphomaniac.

I smiled, thinking to myself that I wish it were true that I had messed up his happy home. I wanted it to be true that that silly little spell I performed decreased his sex drive and that his body was plagued with an illness that she couldn't handle. I was hoping like hell that she would leave him high and dry – just like he left me. Karma.

I wasn't far from the Hilton, so I left my car where I had parked it earlier and walked about a block to the hotel. I figured that I would get some rest and make my way to Arizona in the morning. Besides, I didn't want to go home to my spooky house where I had dabbled in black magic.

My new life was waiting for me. Plus, I didn't want to be near Jacksonville when everyone received the news about being fired. Now – life is grand.

GETHAMBE

I am a natural-born leader. I'm strong, intelligent, and confident with a shitload of attitude. I have no fear or love in my heart. I was bred to be dominant over others, schooled to be direct when speaking, and mastered the art of being mysterious and unpredictable. I am an asshole who never took 'no' for an answer. Things were done my way or no way at all.

I have a serious anger issue, so others know not to piss me off, but I'm a smooth talker when it comes to females. I have the gift of gab, and bitches have no problem giving me that sweet, juicy pussy. However, I don't lick that shit. But I demand that they suck the cum from my dick. I have a lack of respect for authority because I feel that only my opinion counts. So, if I disagree with what someone has to say, I shut them the hell up.

And most importantly, I'm cocky as fuck. I do what I want, to who I want, whenever I want. My mother doesn't even cross me. My father, on the other hand, is a different story. Because we are both bulls, we tend to clash a lot. He's the only being, besides our elders, who can keep my beast at bay – sometimes.

Like most predators, killing came easy for me. Whether it was for food, because you pissed me off, or just for sport – I don't give a damn about taking a life. And because of my predatorial characteristics, tonight, I was going to walk amongst death to become the Alpha of our pack.

The ceremony had to take place tonight while the moon was full. My people have dominated these lands since the beginning of time. No one truly knows the full story of our existence, but our legend states that we are the descendants of Samael, the Archangel of Death, and Lilith, the first Succubus created and one of Samael's wives.

The locals refer to my kind as werewolves, but we are so much more than that. We are officially – Skinwalkers. Once you complete the death ceremony to life, you can morph your being into many other animals. But our wolf is the strongest, so we tend to rely on that one more.

I stood six feet four inches in my human form. My skin is the color of desert sand, my hair is jet black and long, my cheekbones are high, and my physique is muscular–chiseled to perfection. I was every woman's dream but could easily be anyone's nightmare. Loving me came at a cost. To be intimate with my beast, one would have to endure the pain with pleasure. My package was large, and my cum was potent. Although I have had the pleasure of sexing the local human women around these parts, after tonight, I will be confined to the women in our pack. As a matter of fact, my wife has already been chosen for me.

"Are you ready for tonight?" my mother asked. She is

the only woman I have been taught to respect. Not to obey but to respect. She has been around for many years and has been through many life cycles, but now her soul needs rest. After the ceremony is complete, she and my father will join the elders in the Ancient Kingdom of Transjordan. We refer to it as Edom.

"I was born ready," I replied. My voice was strong, my words precise, and my heart revved for the battle that I was to face.

"That's my son," I heard my father announce. "Show no fear, and you shall live forever."

"Now, take off your clothes," my mother told me.

I stripped and was redressed instantly in the ceremonial garments by the Seven Virgins that surrounded me. They would be the offering to satisfy Lilith. She was not able to have children because her womb was cursed for leaving the Garden of Eden. Lilith was Adam's first wife. Because she didn't want to submit to her husband, she ran away and hid in a cave. Legend states that Samael, the Archangel of Death, found her and took her as his first wife.

For gifting us the power of shapeshifting, we would offer her seven virgins to have her babies. Samael then uses his power of temptation to make them sin by whispering the suggestion of becoming 'promiscuous' with the other male fallen angels from Seventh Heaven. As they are sexed, their bodies transform into birthing paraphernalia, and they give birth to many Demi-Demons.

As I walked into the cold cave, dimly lit by torches, I saw the inverted pentagram drawn on the floor with a sacrifice table in its center. At the tip of each point on the star stood Samael, Lilith, Eisheth Zenunim, Na'amah, and Agrat bat Mahlat.

We greeted Samael first. Although he spoke, it wasn't in English, but in the ancient language. He told me to be strong and have faith. As we made our way to Lilith, my mother whispered, "She is an extremely dangerous demon. Don't let her inside of your head."

I looked at my mother and told her, "She should be worried about me. She may be a dangerous succubus, but my dick game is strong." I glanced at my father, who wasn't too happy with my choice of words.

"Niichaad," she spoke. Her voice was angelic, her skin smooth and bronze, and her body petite but voluptuous.

"As you walk around the circle of death, each of Samael's wives will offer you a traditional name. When you return to your pride, you are to choose one of the names offered to you. You will no longer be known as Jacob," my father whispered to me. "Niichaad means, Swollen," he explained.

So, Lilith gave me a name pertaining to my dick; I laughed to myself. It was long, thick, and ready for action. All she had to do was disrobe, and I would rock her eternal world.

I nodded my head and moved around the circle to Samael's youngest wife, Eisheth Zenunim. She looked at me, and I could tell she was digging deep into my soul. She had a wickedness about her that would scare the mortal man. I could see that she was beautiful but deadly.

My mother whispered, "If you fail at being a prominent

leader of this pride, Eisheth will eat your soul and condemn your essence to a life of servitude."

"Atsidi," she whispered. I would have thought of her to be his favorite wife. Eisheth was tall, slender, elegant, with golden-brown skin and electrifying blue eyes. Her hair hung down to her ankles; it was jet black and silky. She was gorgeous.

"Atsidi means Hammer," my mother stated.

Again, I nodded my head and moved around the circle to Na'amah. My mother didn't have to warn me about Na'amah because I could tell she was cold and heartless when I gazed into her eyes. She reminded me of myself.

"Be careful of this one. She sings a pleasing song to make men do whatever her heart desires. Samael is immune to her succubus songs of seduction. But he uses this wife to conquer other realms of the underworld," my father spoke quietly.

"Bidziil," Na'amah spoke. She was beautiful in an evil type of way. To be one of the oldest elders, she carried herself well. Na'amah was curvaceous, her skin as dark as tar, her eyes were as red as fire, and her lips were full and inviting.

"Bidziil means, He is strong," my father informed me.

Lastly, before going to the altar, I went to the final point where the fourth wife stood. Agrat bat Mahlat was the most feminine and beautiful of them all. She was thick in all the right places. Her breasts set high and were full. I could see her nipples as they poked out through her gown. Her ass was firm and perfectly round, and Agrat bat Mahlat's waist was tiny.

"I can hear your thoughts, son," my father said. He knew that I was thinking about ramming my dick deep between her thighs. "She hypnotizes her prey with seductive dances. Once you fall under her spell, she sucks the life from your body and gives your soul to Eisheth Zenunim."

"Tse," she spoke softly, then blew a kiss at me.

"Tse means, Rock," my mother whispered.

I noddle my head and walked to the altar with my parents and the Seven Virgins. Lying on the altar was the woman I would mate with before spilling her blood for the elders. My blood sacrifice was groomed for this moment. Volunteers did this to gain entrance into Edom for themselves and their immediate families. Her family would be rewarded with riches beyond belief, and her parents would become instant nobles. They would never stand at the points of the inverted pentagram like the elders, but when they die and reach the ancient kingdom, they will be inserted into a position in our society as someone important. The man would receive a job such as a lawmaker, priest, doctor, or lawyer, while his wife would live as a socialite.

As I disrobed, the Seven Virgins disrobed. My mother and father stood at the foot and head of the altar and started to chant in unison. From the walls appeared demons and members of our pack who joined in with the chant. I could see as the fire sparked and danced as the chant grew louder. Then it was dead silence.

Lilith walked up to me and handed me a golden goblet filled with a concoction made from the Ancient Kingdom. I knew that it was the resurrection bush that was boiled with ancient herbs and spices. It was the poison that was going to stop my heart from beating. I had to die to go to Edom, where my spirit would battle the fallen angels of the Seven Heavens. If I survive the seven battles of damnation, my soul will rejoin my body, and I will be blessed as the new leader of our pack and receive my shape-shifter abilities.

This was not an ordinary fight; this was seven fights to the death. I will not have any weapons to aid me throughout this journey. I have to rely on my physical strength and wit only. Each fallen angel has a weakness, and as my beast grows in power, I will become stronger and wiser, finding the fault they hide within themselves. Also, with each fallen angel that I defeat, I become closer to my Yogi.

Gaining my Yogi will help me to understand and manipulate the laws of nature. It will bring my beast health, power, knowledge, wisdom, and happiness. Yogi is what gives our beast the ability to survive. It's like an inner strength that keeps your aura in tune with the five elements of life: Earth, water, fire, air, and space.

Lilith circled me as if I was her prey, sniffing the air that engulfed my body, then – without warning, she began to massage my manhood. Her hands were as soft as silk and her stroke as slow as molasses. With the slightest movement of her hand, my dick throbbed and pulsated with want.

"Drink," she commanded. "Then mount your prize and take her life."

With each sip of death, I could feel my body warm, and my muscles vibrate. The room began to spin, and my breathing and heart rate slowed. I could hear the chant clearly, although no one was moving their lips.

We invoke thee, our king, our protector.
We worship him, blessed by our elder kin.
Give us death, grant us life.
Out of the darkness and into the light.

Then, the room slowed. I felt drowsy and struggled to regain my bearings as the room began whirring wildly in a blur. Lilith led me to the table and opened the sheer, white gown that my sacrifice wore. She seductively sashayed back to her place, and I watched her eagerly drink in the view of the beautiful creature that was waiting for me to mount her and take her virginity. I then turned my attention to the gorgeous woman lying on the table. To entice me to take her, she ran her hand down between her breasts, to her stomach, and between her thighs where her pearl was hidden.

My mother used her hands to firmly spread her legs apart while my father stood at her head with a gold dagger in his hand.

"Show no fear," he spoke thunderously.

I looked into her soft, hazel eyes and became captivated by her innocence. But my pity for her naïve beauty only lasted seconds. My beast wanted her, and so did I. So, I mounted the beautiful virgin and thrusted into her mercilessly with the power of Zeus. Her body resisted me, and she tried to pull away, but I grabbed her by the neck and steadied my stride as I began to pump savagely into her tightened core.

Once I was totally submerged into her creamy center, I felt her sweetness hug my enormous manhood like a

Chinese finger trap. My dick began lusting for more of her – I wanted to feel her tightness throb and squeeze around my heated rod, begging desperately for the satisfaction of a good, hard fuck.

As I pushed deep into her core forcefully, visions of the Seven Virgins filled my head. I saw that they too were engaged in a ferocious battle of sex and passionate lust with a multitude of men. I watched as the Virgins took turns sucking and riding the men one after another, being used in every orifice imaginable. It made my blood race; I felt excited – jubilant.

When I looked down onto my beautiful sacrifice, I could see her lust for me shimmering in her eyes. I could tell that she was now enjoying the feeling of my dick as it swelled, thumping viciously inside of her. I smiled evilly, relishing how easily I had turned the virgin's innocence to debased, lewd lust. Without noticing, I found that I had wrapped my hand tightly around her neck and had begun shoving the entire length of my shaft – to the hilt – in and out of her wetness.

Her body was as hot as fire and glowing like the bright sun. Her eyes were half shut, and she was squealing uncontrollably in euphoria.

"Take me!" I heard her soft voice scream out.

I felt my balls tighten as my heart was beating fiercely against my chest. The sacrifice's pussy felt so good wrapped tightly around my dick. It took every ounce of my willpower to prevent myself from spilling my seed inside of her. My father placed the dagger in my hand and yelled, "NOW!"

Gripping the dagger, I lifted my arm high into the air. I

looked into the virgin's eyes and resisted the pleading, sorrowful look she gave me. I let my arm come down onto her chest like an unrelenting thunderstorm. Blood shot out of her body like a fountain.

Then, my heart stopped. What killed her – killed me. When I took her life, I gave mine as retribution.

I felt my soul leave my body and begin the epic journey to Edom, where I started the seven battles. As my spirit left, I saw the four wives begin their ritual dance around the altar, playing blissfully in the virgin's blood.

I looked around and watched as the Seven Virgins' tummies swelled instantly, becoming pregnant. Within seconds, they had given birth to Lilith's children. She wasted no time gathering her babies and nestling them into her bosom.

As my soul floated away, everyone disappeared, and my surroundings became dark. I was guided through the afterlife by a being that I couldn't see. When there was light, I was faced with my first battle. My soul was in Seventh Heaven, and my destination was First Heaven. Only there would I gain my Yogi and become an enlightened, supreme deity.

The fight begins.

LANA

I am Lana Yazzie, the firstborn daughter of Pax and Cherish Yazzie. I am next in line to become the Alfa Female of this pack. But like my future husband, I must be evaluated. I need to exhibit the traits of a strong leader. I need to show that I am brave, intelligent, and disciplined, along with being humble and caring.

I was chosen by the elders because of my immense beauty and unique aura. I have the gift of healing my people through touch if they have not passed to the afterlife.

I am tall and slender with smooth copper skin. I have bone-straight, long, black hair and high cheekbones. Although I have a small frame, the gods have blessed me with full breasts, a firm ass, and a small waist. I am just as beautiful inside as I am on the outside but deadly when I need to be.

My first task at hand is to fight a member of our Canine Crew. They are the part of our pack that protects our borders, keeping other predators from reaching our dens. Although it's cloaked, our enemies attack daily, trying to find a weakness. We are in a bitter battle for land. We have it, and they want it.

Each member of the Canine Crew has studied for years in the art of combat. They are fearless, heartless, and stone-cold killers. The chosen ones are taken from their parents at a young age and trained sixteen hours a day until they reach their twenty-first birthday. Then, they are placed in the field as an apprentice with a mentor for the next four years. That is how they learn the ways of a warrior.

As I stood at the entrance of the arena, I allowed a moment of weakness. I felt my heart flutter once or twice with fear. But as I inhaled the fresh air and exhaled the fear, I was ready.

When the door opened, I walked through it slowly and glanced around. An unsettling quietness surrounded my being, and hundreds of eyes were staring down at me. But I held my head up high and made my way to the throne where my elder king and queen sat.

I had an advantage over my rival because I not only had the same training, but I had intimate knowledge of our people's ways. I knew their strengths and their weaknesses. They were mindless soldiers who were used to taking orders, not making calculated decisions. Our generals were responsible for planning out our attacks, and it was the job of the pack to execute their orders. They were used to fighting as one unit, where I was taught to manipulate the mind to conquer the body.

I walked up to the golden thrones that were placed in the middle of the stadium. King Jabari and Queen Ebonee sat there with their heads held high, their faces emotionless, and their disposition – sheer power.

King Jabari held a golden staff in his hand that he used to tap the ground three times. I bowed, showing respect to my elder king and his queen before turning to face my opponent.

The large wooden doors opened, and my competition appeared. She was a large woman in height and size. Fatima was battle-ready; her face was as cold as ice, her eyes filled with hatred, and she wore the coat of fearless demeanor.

She entered the arena, raising her shield and sword as she ran laps around it. Her stride was masculine and roaring, exciting the pack. Their howls engulfed the stadium, causing an unsettling vibration throughout my body. These were her friends, people she worked closely with. So, I understood as they applauded her pre-victorious battle cry. But I stood firm and studied her intimately, looking for a weakness. I couldn't hone in on one; she was faultless.

I pulled my hair up, braided it to the end, and wrapped it into a sloppy knot. I picked up my shield, engraved with my family's crest, and my steel sword, given to my family by the Archangel Gabrielle many moons ago. Then I positioned my body in an attack stance and waited for Fatima to make her move.

I watched, listened, and studied our surroundings and anticipated her next move. She charged me and jumped five feet off the ground. As her heavy body began to fall onto me, I lifted my shield to block her incoming blow. Her hit was a lightning blow, striking my shield and knocking my body backward. I dug my feet into the ground, trying to brace for the impact, but I was being propelled back by her thunderous hit, leaving a trail in the sand.

She retreated and began to circle me like I was her prey. I could hear her growling as she rounded me; each time, her voice became louder. We did this to scare our opponents but hearing this struck no fear into my heart.

Realizing that she had not accomplished her goal of rattling my nerves, she came toward me swinging her sword. When she reached me, our swords clashed, the hit sounding like two trains colliding. She swayed her sword fiercely, clashing it with mine as I blocked her attacks. We spun, we ducked, and we thrusted our swords, trying to penetrate the heart of the other opponent. Our bodies twisted and turned as if we were participating in a bitter bolero dance.

Her sword flew over my head, missing me by mere inches. I knew then that I had to end this battle quickly. So, I thrusted my sword into her side, piercing Fatima's skin, causing blood to trickle down it. With her new wound, the pack began to howl and thump their feet against the ground, shaking the Earth and waking the spirits.

She backed away slowly, reassessing the situation. But I didn't give her time to think. I ran toward her, and as she lifted her shield, I slid on the ground between her legs. I raised my sword and sliced her inner thigh. Fatima fell to her knees, dropping her shield and sword to the ground.

The pack grew silent, watching for me to make my next move. I looked up at my elder king and queen with blood lust in my eyes. They looked at me but didn't give me any hint of what they were thinking.

So, I dropped my shield, walked up behind my opponent while she kneeled wounded on her knees, and grabbed a fist full of her hair. I pulled her head backward and exposed her neck. Fatima knew that she was about to die, but she still showed no fear. She did not cry or beg for her life. She remained firm as the Angel of Death danced around her body. Her face was stern, and her heart was hardened.

Instead of slicing her neck from ear to ear, I tossed my sword to the side and released my grip on her hair. I walked around Fatima and kneeled in front of her. I leaned in and placed one hand on her side and the other on her inner thigh. I closed my eyes and chanted the song of healing that my mother had taught me many years ago. My hands illuminated bright gold, lighting up the entire area where we were kneeling, face to face. Within seconds, her cuts were mended.

As I removed my hands from her body, a crushing force shot through me. My body began to levitate into the air as the Eye of Horus was etched on my right shoulder. The burning sensation caused me to scream out in pain. My entire body was on fire, but there was only one tattoo being engraved onto me.

When my body descended to the ground, I felt an overwhelming feeling of serenity. My senses had sharpened, allowing me to hear the heartbeat of nearby prey. My sense of smell was intensified, permitting me to smell the blood of the humans that lived near our den. And my eyesight was that of a hawk. I could see everything.

As I tried to balance myself out from all the changes, King Jabari and Queen Ebonee approached me. When

King Jabari placed his hand onto my shoulder, my body morphed into my beast.

"You have attained your Yogi, my child," he said.

"Because you showed mercy to your opponent, the elders have blessed you," Queen Ebonee stated.

"Now, you need to become one with your beast," King Jabari said. Then King Jabari looked at the pack in the stadium. "You are all dismissed. Lana and her family need time alone," he announced, tapping his staff against the ground three times. Within seconds, the colosseum was emptied except for my mother, father, and Fatima, who was still kneeling on the ground.

My parents morphed into their wolves to teach me the ways of the beast. Although we were not in human form, we were able to communicate telepathically. As long as one could transform into their beast, they could talk to other members without using the verbal language.

"When she has finished her first stage of training, you need to escort her to our quarters for the second phase of becoming Jacob's wife. She needs to be at one with her beast before he awakens, so spare no time," King Jabari commanded, leaving us and walking over to Fatima.

He looked down at her with disgust. We all knew that she was about to be expelled from the pack because she lost her battle to me. What made it worse for her was, I spared her life and healed her battle wounds.

Fatima was supposed to die a warrior's death. But I had known her since we were children and couldn't take her life. She was a good fighter; I just had the advantage. She was only taught to kill, but I was taught to think about the situation before attacking. My mother always used to tell me, *"Only a fool runs into a fight without knowing how to defeat his enemy. Be patient and wait for them to show you their weakness."*

Fatima didn't realize that when she backed away from me to assess her wound, she left herself wide open for me to attack. Now, she will pay for her mistake with her life. Once she leaves the pack, our enemies will catch and kill her.

My king and queen left, leaving my parents to teach me about my beast and explain the new tattoo on my shoulder. I noticed that only those who could transform had the Eye of Horus marking. Only King Jabari's body displayed more tattoos than I could count. One day I'm sure that will be explained to me too.

It only took my parents a couple of hours to teach me how to command my beast. I learned that I was able to transform into a wolf, a hawk, and an owl. My wolf was my strength, my hawk was my eyes to see over distant lands, and my owl was my ears. I was the ultimate being under the elders. But I was warned about the misuse of my Yogi. Right now, my body was in tune with the five elements of life. But, to keep them in a harmonic balance, I could not do wrong for my personal gain. If the elders saw that I was misusing my Yogi, they would come down from the Seven Heavens and condemn my soul into an everlasting burning Hell.

After training, my mother walked me into the royal quarters, where I would learn how to please my husband. She kissed me on the forehead before leaving and told me how proud I had made her.

As she turned to walk out the door, Queen Ebonee motioned for me to come to her. I walked into her domicile and bowed. "Stand my child," she said; her voice was soft and angelic.

"I'm here to learn how to be a good wife to Jacob," I replied, watching as my queen approached me, draped in a beautiful sheer gown.

I could not believe that she was over five hundred years old – her body was exquisite, unmatched by any other I had laid my eyes on. I couldn't help but obsess over how gorgeous she truly was. Her skin was a smooth, silky ivory and her hair was jet black, tumbling down to her waist. Her eyes were dark but inviting, and her breasts were small, round, but full. Her posterior was firm, tight, and commanded attention. She was the very definition of perfection.

"To be the wife of a king, you have to perfect your role as his queen," she began as she circled her chamber, lighting the white candles that surrounded it. "You have to know when to speak and what to say...you must never cross him or go against his word," she explained. "Even when you think he's wrong...you will tell the pack that he is right."

As she finished lighting her candles, she looked at me.

"But know that a king is only as good as his queen," she finished, unbuttoning her gown, and allowing it to slide off her body and onto the floor.

"Yes, ma'am," I agreed dutifully.

I knew that she spoke the truth because no one in this pack had ever heard King Jabari or Queen Ebonee argue. His word has always been final.

"Finally, you must understand the sexual desire of a man. Know that he will not only desire you. It's the nature of his beast. He will also have a deep longing for other women in this pack," she warned me, laying across the bed and spreading her legs wide. "You must understand that those other women mean nothing...because *you* are his queen. They are only his playthings, nothing more. Sex is meant for his enjoyment – not for yours."

"So, when my husband finally makes love to me, will I not enjoy it?" I questioned.

"When Jacob takes your virginity, it is going to feel like he's ripping your insides apart. He is going to be brutal, and the act itself will be savage. Like you, all his senses will be heightened. When he feels your sweetness wrapped around his manhood, he is going to be driven insane with lust," she said, motioning for a younger servant girl to come to her.

She looked at the young woman with desire dancing in her eyes. Understanding, the young servant girl disrobed instantly. As if she had done this so many times before, she swiftly climbed into the bed with my queen and began to lick her pearl, slowly and sensually. I watched my queen as she swirled her hips seductively, riding her tongue in lust.

"*Mmmmmh*," I heard her moan. "When looking for gratification for yourself, you have many chambermaids to choose from. But never defile your body with another man – he may never enter your hallowed sanctuary. That is for your husband only."

I could see that she was finding it harder to get her words out. Queen Ebonee was enjoying her slow descent into euphoria with every swirl of her hips. The young servant girl's head was bobbing quickly, trying to keep up the pace, desperately trying to get my queen to her destination.

Queen Ebonee tilted her head backward and arched her back. Her hips were swirling quickly, and her breathing became heavy as she howled loudly, as if she was in the presence of a full moon.

"Yes. Yes. *Yes*," she screamed out as her cream shot against the face of her servant. Without the queen asking, the servant girl crawled off the bed, grabbed a damp cloth, and began to clean the queen. When Queen Ebonee had been sufficiently attended to, she quietly wiped her face off. Redressing herself, she stood quietly against the wall with her head lowered, her face turning a gentle shade of pink. I could understand her shyness; I was embarrassed, and it wasn't even me eating Queen Ebonee out.

"So, the pleasure I receive will come from my servant girls and not my husband?" I asked. "Will my husband not be unhappy with my infidelities? Even if they are women?"

"He will know, and he will understand," the queen said curtly.

She slipped off the bed and approached me, still naked.

"If Jacob just so happens to hit *that* spot and it makes you climax, thank the Gods for that moment because it won't happen often. The primary purpose of sex with him is reproduction – to give him a son to continue his legacy. So, you will mate with him often, you will obey his command, and you will never cross your husband. You will remain blind to his indiscretions, and you will only give your opinion when he asks for it. We are to be seen, not heard," she said solemnly. "Now, leave me. My husband will be arriving any minute," she finished, turning her back to me.

I bowed and left my queen's chambers, passing King Jabari on my way out. He looked at me and smiled wickedly.

It must be nice to be a king, I thought to myself.

"It is," he answered, going into the queen's chambers.

In the heat of my encounter with Queen Ebonee, I had forgotten that we were all connected through our beast. In order to keep the pack from hearing my thoughts, I had to flip the mental switch in my beast's consciousness.

My fiancé would be returning to me shortly, and I had to prepare myself for the marriage ceremony. Although I have trained for this moment all my life, I still wasn't prepared for what I was about to embrace. I wasn't afraid. But I was a tad bit nervous.

4

ASHLEY

I had to get out of this damn house. I don't know what the fuck is going on, but all night long, I hear those damn wolves howling. It freaks me out at times because they sound as if they are right outside of my home. This shit has been going on for about a week, and my nerves are fucking shot.

So, tonight I'm going out on a blind date. Although I'm not ready to get back into the dating scene, I let my loneliness get the best of me. After I first arrived, my phone rang nonstop. People back home were pissed because I had them all fired. But they deserved it. All those backstabbing hoes walked around for months, smiling in my face while they were laughing behind my back. The way I felt, they all got what they fucking deserved. Now I'm the bitch laughing at them.

The one cousin I know here was fixing me up with her husband's friend. I wouldn't say I liked the fact that he is supposed to be a single father who was actively raising his young son and daughter. I'm not the one to deal with that baby momma drama shit. For one, I have too much class to stoop to her level. For two, I'm too damn old to be fighting some bitch over a man. Especially when there are so many of them for me to choose from. Because I'm loaded with money, independent as hell, and sexy, I would never have a problem grabbing the attention of any man.

As I fumbled through my closet looking for the right outfit to wear, I heard those damn wolves starting to howl again. It seems that they are getting louder and louder every night. But, I love to look my best, and first impressions are everything. I'm going to rush myself and pull this style together. I don't want to leave the house in the late evening, just in case the wolves are hungry. Because my beauty is so captivating, I know I look good enough to eat.

I found a cute blue jumpsuit with white stripes and a bow under the breasts. I purchased this outfit a couple of months ago but never wore it. It didn't show too much but showed enough to catch any man's eye.

I took a quick shower and slipped into my clothes. I pulled my hair up into a high ponytail, lined my eyes, and applied a gorgeous pink lip gloss that shimmered with the slightest bit of light. To set my look off, I wore some big, silver hoop earrings and a couple of silver bracelets. I slid into a pair of sandals, grabbed my Bvlgari shoulder bag, and headed for my car.

As I walked out of the door, I noticed that the sun was beginning to hide itself behind the rigid mountains. The sky was beautifully decorated with vibrant colors of crimson red, magenta, and burnt orange. Seeing that romantic sky made me realize how much I wanted to be a part of someone's, anyone's life. I missed being held at night and kissed in the morning. I missed having that companionship with the one person in the world who gave you that unconditional love. I missed feeling loved.

I made my way to the car only to hear those wolves howling like they were in a pack and searching for their next meal. Because it sent unsettling shivers racing throughout my body, I hurried my stride and jumped into my car. Although I knew they couldn't open my car doors, I locked them so that I felt a little safer. I raced down the long dirt driveway to the main street and made my way into the city to meet my date.

When I sped into the parking lot of the Bahama Café, I realized that I was not going to be afforded the luxurious dining atmosphere I was accustomed to. I'm the type of woman who loves exotic food and expensive wine; however, this was a hole-in-the-wall restaurant where thugs met up after a drive-by. It was in a historic building that needed some serious renovations, and it sat next to a dairy farm. So, I don't think I need to tell you how bad it smelled. Just the thought of me eating from an establishment so filthy made my stomach churn like butter. I was sickened just getting out of my damn car. *What type of small-town hick shit have I gotten myself into?* I thought to myself as I grabbed my bag and headed for the door.

I approached the door and was scared to touch the handle to pull it open. All I could see were germs swimming all over it. To avoid catching the swine flu or something a doctor couldn't cure, I stood to the side and waited for someone to open it for me. People could say what they wanted about me, but I wasn't used to this shit.

Looking around the restaurant, I tried to find my date. My cousin said that he was a darker-skinned man with a fantastic body. I believe her words were something like, "You will know him when you see him."

"Ashley?" I heard a strong, deep, masculine voice say.

I turned around to face the voice, and I must admit, my cousin was absolutely right. He was tall, dark, and extremely handsome. His physique was muscular, and his smile was attractive with those thick lips and heavenly white teeth. He was everything she said he would be and more.

"Yes," I exhaled with passion.

"I'm Kwan," he announced. "I'm the blind date," he smiled.

I was lost in his sexy dark eyes as I floated on a sea of desire. He was so good-looking that I was at a loss for words. All I could do was stare at this mind-blowing beast that was sent to me by the Egyptian Gods.

"Ashley," I heard him say.

"Oh, forgive me," I said, trying to excuse my behavior. "Yes, I'm Ashley," I smiled.

"It seems that I'm a little underdressed for the occasion," he laughed.

I giggled, but it wasn't sincere because I was still at a loss for words. This man was mesmerizing, and his good looks clouded my judgment. "You're fine. I had this old thing for years; it's nothing special," I lied. This outfit was new and had cost me a pretty penny.

"Let's grab a seat," he suggested, placing his hand in the small of my back and guiding me to a table that was snuggled in the corner of the restaurant. He pulled out my chair and assisted me by pushing it back under the table after I sat down. That was a true gentlemanly quality. Something that a lot of men lacked.

He sat across from me and picked up the menu. I picked up mine to see what type of food this hideous place offered. As I glanced over it, I couldn't fathom eating anything from it. They served the kind of food that caused heart attacks and diabetes. The only thing I wanted was a glass of water. And judging by the dirty spoon on my table, I was hoping and praying that even that came in a bottle.

"Tell me about yourself," I said, folding the menu back up and placing it back onto the table.

"Well, I'm sure you know I have two kids that live at home with me. Justin is ten, and Justice is eight. I work for Ridgecrest Nursing Facility as their administrator. I have only been married once; Tamar was my high school sweetheart, but we divorced after she started using drugs," he explained. "Now it's your turn."

"Okay," I smiled. "I just moved here from Jacksonville, Florida. I am newly divorced, and I don't have children. There's really not much that I could tell you; besides, I'm looking for a fresh start."

"Fresh start, huh?" he questioned.

"Yes. I'm hoping to find love again, but this time I'm not going to rush it. I want to move slow and allow myself to get to know my next husband," I smiled.

He looked at me so seductively that I could feel my

lady throb in want. This man made my heart skip beats with every word that spilled from his mouth. I didn't even know him, but I felt comfortable talking to him. His personality shone like the sun, warming the entire room. The way he was so attentive to me gave me a false sense of security.

He licked his lips and asked, "I'm going to have the smothered pork chops and mashed potatoes. What would you like?"

"I'm not hungry," I lied. My stomach was craving food, any food. But I just couldn't bring myself to eat anything from this grimy ass place.

"I know what you're thinking," he laughed. "I was the same way when I first ate here. This place may not look clean, but it is, and the food is superb."

I batted my eyes at him and responded with a devilish smile, "Whatever do you mean?"

We both burst out laughing, causing the other people in the restaurant to glance over at our table.

"Trust me on this. I wouldn't lead you astray," he guaranteed.

"Okay then. I will have what you are having," I said as he motioned for a waiter to come to our table.

Kwan ordered our food, and we continued to get to know each other. I found him to be extremely interesting and intelligent. I began to admire him for taking on the single-parent role. As much as we talked about his children, I felt as though I had already met them. I learned so much about him within the couple of hours that we had spent together. And the food was fabulous. I wished they offered a less fattening menu, but he was right about its taste regardless of the calorie intake I suffered.

As the night concluded, he walked me to my car. "I had a wonderful time," I acknowledged.

"I had a wonderful time as well," he agreed. "So, do you live close?" he asked.

"I'm not too far from here," I answered. "I live on the border of Winslow and the Navajo reservation."

"Okay," he said. "You like that solitude lifestyle," he joked.

"Not as much as you think. I had inherited some land from my great-grandmother, who was Navajo. So, while I was going through my divorce, I had a home built there," I said, getting into my car. "The only thing is, for about the last week or so, the wolves keep howling. It's like I have a pack of them right outside of my house. And their howls are bone-chilling and scary," I confessed.

"Why don't you stay in town for a couple of days?" he asked. "I'm sure your cousin would allow you to stay a few nights with her until the wolves calm down."

Now, I don't have anything against my cousin, but I can't stay at her home knowing that her husband will be there while she's at work. I was taught that you never bring a single woman into a married household. Besides, they have too many children running around that little ass house. I like my space and privacy. Not to mention my vibrators that kept my body satisfied during my dry spell.

"I'm sure she would welcome me with open arms," I smiled. "But I think I'm just going to grab a hotel room for the night and drive home in the morning."

"I know of a charming hotel if you want to follow me over there. I have to go in that direction anyway."

I felt like I knew where this was going, but I was okay with it. He wanted to test the waters of my sweetness. I haven't been with a man since before my miscarriage. It would be nice to have a man to blow my back out. I'm just hoping like hell that his dick is good, and his stroke game puts me to sleep.

"Sure," I answered. He shut my door and went to his car. I followed him through the city of Winslow to a well-lit hotel. He pulled into the hotel and parked his vehicle first as if he knew that I would ask him to join me for an intimate encounter.

I pulled up beside him and turned my car off. I got out and walked over to his car and knocked on the window. He was on his cell phone, perhaps talking to his children and letting them know that he would either be home later or that he would be home in the morning.

I stood there for only a few seconds before walking away. I lack patience. That quality has never been one of my strengths.

Seeing me walk away from his car made him change his tune because he caught up with me before I got to the door. "I'm sorry about that," he said.

"That's okay. I understand. But I don't stand around and wait for anyone for anything," I said in my sweet, innocent voice. I wasn't trying to scare him away before seeing what type of package he had to offer. Hell, my body needed this. And even if he doesn't have a big dick, he could use his tongue for something other than talking.

As I approached the desk, Kwan advised me that he would be paying for my room. He was kind enough to pay for dinner and now for a place to stay. He was so kind and adorable. I was really feeling Kwan's gentlemanly demeanor.

He talked to the clerk and obtained the key to the room. Kwan looked at the key and then at me. I think he was waiting for his official invitation. Being forward is not a part of my personality when it comes to sexual adventures. That is the only time I demand a man to be dominant.

Since he was too chicken shit to say anything, I politely took the key from his hand and thanked him for his Southern hospitality. He got with the game when I started to walk away. "Would you like some company for a couple of hours?" he asked.

"Now, Kwan," I whispered, turning to look at his handsome face and amazing physique. "Are you trying to come to my room so that you can sample my goodies?"

He looked at me and grinned. "Yes, ma'am, I am," he answered honestly. "I have been thinking about being between those thighs all evening."

"I might let you taste it," I said, walking back over to him and pulling him to me by his shirt. "Would you like to taste it?" I inquired.

"Yes, ma'am," he answered.

I released his shirt and repositioned it on his body. "Then follow me," I instructed. I know it's wrong to sleep with a man you barely know, but my lady is crying out for a bit of attention. And being the gracious owner that I am, I'm going to give her what she wants.

We made our way to the room, and I opened the door. I walked in and flipped the light switch on. Kwan was quick on my heels and *way too* eager to get down to business. He was unzipping his pants as he was shutting the door and was damn near hopping on one foot as he tried to get out of his damn clothes.

"Slow down," I laughed. "We don't have to rush through this."

"I'm not trying to rush, Baby. I'm just a little excited," he smiled back.

I laid my bag down on the small table and sat on the bed, watching him undress. I was eager to see what he was packing any damn way.

My eyes bored into him like a hawk as he pulled his boxers down. When they hit the floor, I was highly fucking disappointed.

I thought to myself, *this is going to be a waste of my motherfucking time.* Don't get me wrong, his dick was fat, but it lacked length. He may fill me up, but he definitely wasn't going to be hitting any of my walls or bottoming out. I felt like this son-of-a-bitch had pulled a Houdini trick on me because the dick I had been expecting had magically disappeared.

What the fuck?

Thoroughly disappointed, I stood up and pulled off my cute little jumpsuit. As he lay across the bed massaging his dick, I slid out of my panties first, then unsnapped my bra and let it drop to the floor. I walked over to where he was lying and crawled into the bed.

"You said you wanted to taste it," I reminded him as I stood up in the bed and over him.

"Bring that pussy to me," he demanded, running his hands up and down my legs. Although I knew this man couldn't possibly satisfy my deepest desires, I relented. Kneeling, I sat myself down onto his face.

He grabbed my ass, pulling me firmly onto his lips. Passionately, he sucked on my lady, surprising me with his fervent want. I slid my hips forward and backward, rotating them slowly as I rode his tongue like a surfboard. I grabbed my taut nipples and began to pinch and tug on them, igniting a small fire of excitement in the pit of my stomach.

His juicy lips and soft tongue sent waves of arousal racing through me. I could feel my body become excited, and small spurts of my cream began to spill from my sweet core onto his face.

"*Uhmmm*," I moaned, enjoying the sensuality of the moment.

To add a little pain to my pleasure, I felt Kwan delicately place one finger into my rosebud and begin to finger-fuck it gently.

As he licked, nibbled, and laved my sensitive nub, the pace of my thrusts against him quickened. The feeling of his tongue running up and down my clit, searching, prodding, and tasting was nothing short of exquisite.

I had reached the point where I felt like I could spurt my sweet juices into his mouth, but not knowing him well enough, a sense of self-conscious embarrassment stopped me. Considerately but reluctantly, I pulled back off his lips and let my body calm.

"I want to be inside of you," he whispered.

"Do you have a condom?" I asked. Honestly, I didn't think he had enough dick to put into one, but I definitely wanted to play it safe, just in case he did.

"Yeah, right here," he answered.

I pulled my body off his and allowed him to retrieve the condom from his pants pocket. I couldn't help but think about how fine this man was but disappointed about how little he had to offer. The only thing that he had going for himself was his *incredible* tongue action.

Somehow, he managed to slide a condom on his stubby little dick and have it fit. I lay on my back and opened my legs wide for him. Kwan crawled between my thighs and inserted himself into my tightness. He wasted no time, beginning to hammer into my sweetness almost instantly. Unexpectedly, I felt him inside me! I mean, I think I did. To be honest, it felt like we were bumping pussies. I could barely feel anything.

"Kwan," I whispered in his ear. "Let me close my legs."

"Okay, okay," he huffed, with sweat dripping off his forehead as he worked overtime to have me feel him inside of me.

I closed my legs and squeezed my pelvis. This way, I knew my clit would at least get some of the action. Barely letting up, he resumed pounding my pussy like a hammer on a nail. Now, however, I could feel that small fire begin to burn inside of me again. This didn't feel half bad! No, he wasn't going as deep as I needed, but the sensation of having his tiny manhood sliding gracefully across my nub was quite delightful.

I thrust my hips up and down to maximize the contact between us, and I felt my clit begin to throb in anticipation. I could feel my lady swell, aching for a sweet release.

Kwan was working hard, bless his big heart and tiny dick. His eyes were closed, and he was biting down onto his bottom lip as he pumped, trying his absolute best to fulfill both our needs with the earnest vigor of a teenage schoolboy.

Between my legs, I could feel his dick thump with excitement. I closed my eyes and imagined that he was someone else – anyone else – with a monster dick that could satisfy a nation. With that, I pushed my hips up to meet his as he thrusted downward into me. Feeling him stimulate my lady sent a flood of tingling vibrations throughout my body. My heart was thudding uncontrollably, my body trembling with jubilation as my lady yearned to be set free.

As I felt the warm gush squirt from my body, I gasped for air. Kwan continued to push between my legs, but I laid perfectly still as I enjoyed my slow and elegant descent into a euphoric bliss.

"FUUUUCK!" he yelled, reaching his climax. His body was bucking wildly as he emptied his seed into the condom. "You got some good shit!" he groaned, slowly pulling out of me.

How would he know? It felt like the tip of his dick didn't get much further than my lady's opening. Yeah, maybe it was because my thighs were thick. But personally, I know it was because his penis was a bit insufficient to handle a woman like me.

I gently pushed him off me and got out of the bed.

"Baby," he said. "Where are you going?" he asked.

"I'm going to take a shower," I replied. "You can wash up in the sink, and I'm sure you remember where the door is. Let yourself out when you're finished."

"You want me to leave?" he asked, sounding confused.

As I stated earlier, my tongue is sharp, and you can't ever say that you didn't understand the words that fell elegantly from these lips. So, I stated in a slow and degrading tone, "Kwan. You're sexy; that much is true. But you don't have enough dick to keep a woman like me happy," I said, my disdain for him dripping from each word I spoke. "Sweetheart, you didn't even get to feel this sweet pussy wrapped around you. Your little ass dick only played with my clit. We can be friends, and I would love for you to eat my pussy again. But as far as us kicking it daily, it's just not going to happen."

Kwan threw a temper tantrum as he gathered his things. He called me a couple of bitches before storming out of the room. It didn't matter, though; I got what I needed.

I took a quick shower and snuggled myself comfortably into the bed. I had had my fun, and now, my body was exhausted – I did do most of the work after all. I pulled the comforter up to my chin and quickly fell into a deep sleep.

GETHAMBE

I had won six of the seven battles, and now my spirit was ascending to First Heaven. I was mentally drained but prepared for whatever the Gods had waiting for me. As my body floated through the darkness and into the light, I felt an overwhelming sense of tranquility. Unlike the other six Heavens, my soul felt welcomed, and the golden rays of sunshine washed away all the stress of these battles.

"Welcome," I heard a booming voice say. But as I looked around, I saw nothing but puffy white clouds and dancing bright stars. There was no one there but me. "Come through the golden gates," he said. As I looked toward the direction where I heard the voice, a giant golden gate appeared before my very eyes.

I walked over to them and pushed them open. As I walked through them, the light became brighter, blinding me. I tried to hold my hand up to block the brightness, but it barely helped. I could see a dark figure walking toward me, but I couldn't determine who or what it was. But the closer it got to me, the more at ease my body became. This deity was inviting and cast an extreme peace over the area.

"Return home and care for your people Jacob. They are going to need a strong leader like yourself," he said. His voice was angelic, loving, and accepting.

"Who are you?" I asked, thinking this was another trick from one of the archangels.

"I am who I am," he announced, touching me on my shoulder.

Then the light faded, and I could feel my soul being pulled downward. I was falling fast, passing scenes of my epic battles with each archangel. This wasn't making sense to me. I was denied the right to finish my last fight, and my family would be punished for my failure.

Just as I thought that all hope had failed, my soul was plunged back into my body, and I jumped up and exhaled a hideous howl. It was loud and shook the mountains and the ground.

I looked around and saw my pack, my parents, and what was to be my new wife. Before I could address anyone, my body was lifted high into the sky as tattoos were being burned into my skin.

The first tattoo that I recognized was the Eye of Horus. It is an ancient symbol of protection and good health. It fuels the beast within me. Another one that was being etched into my skin was the symbol of Ankh. This was the key of life that balanced my beast with the five elements of my Yogi. And the last one I recognized was the Eye of Ra that was being burned onto the back of my hand. This was another symbol of protection, but it gave me valuable insight into the rite of passage. With that, I was able to move between realms.

Other etchings were being burned into my body, but I didn't know what they represented or why my body was being marked up like a tablet. I was sure that these ancient markings would be explained to me once the Gods were through burning them onto my body.

The pain I endured as the fire burned tattoo after tattoo into my skin was intolerable. But there was no stopping it, and a man wasn't allowed to cry, especially not the future king. Showing such an emotion displayed weakness. And that was something I was not.

As the last tattoo was etched onto me, my body began to descend back down onto the altar. But it had changed from when I last saw it. The pentagram was upright, the sacrificial volunteer's body was gone, and everything was white. There was a heavy odor of herbs and spices that engulfed the air that surrounded me. Everything seemed to be pure, innocent, and reclaimed by God himself.

I sat on the side of the altar with my tattoos emanating a dull gold light from them. I was confused and unaware of the elders standing against the cavern wall watching my every movement. My body ached, and I was exhausted. All I wanted was for someone to allow me to sleep.

As the glowing from my tattoos subsided, my father approached me. I could see the contentment in his eyes. Whatever happened, I knew that I had made him a proud man. My father wasn't the emotional type, but he wrapped his arms around me with pride when I was reborn. He held me close to him as if this was the first time he had seen my face.

"Have you chosen a name?" The Archangel Samael asked.

I remembered that each demon wife suggested names, but none of those names gave meaning to the king I was soon to be.

"Gethambe," I answered.

"Can he do that?" Lilith asked; her voice was spiteful and harsh. "No one has ever broken our tradition before," she stated.

"Gethambe?" Samael asked.

"Somewhere amongst the heavens, I heard someone whisper to me that name. They said to me that I would be a powerful king. And Gethambe means, source of great power," I answered.

Samael thought about it while his wives argued. They had named every king, named every successor, and every first-born daughter that was given to Lilith as an appreciation gift. And it angered them that I was not willing to accept a name they offered me.

"Silence!" he yelled to his wives. His voice was solid and earth-shattering. "Gethambe, you shall be called," he announced.

I stood up, and everyone within my pack bowed to me. They chanted the Serenity Prayer by Reinhold Niebuhr:

God grant me the serenity
to accept the things I cannot change;
courage to change the things I can;

56

And wisdom to know the difference.
Living one day at a time;
enjoying one moment at a time;
accepting hardships as the pathway to peace;
taking, as He did, this sinful world
as it is, not as I would have it;
trusting that He will make all things right
if I surrender to His Will;
that I may be reasonably happy in this life
and supremely happy with Him
Forever in the next.
Amen.

As they finished, my father removed the necklace from around his neck and placed it around mine. It was the family crest; two wolves intertwined. It represented life, love, peace, and prosperity.

"After your marriage ceremony tonight, this land will become your land. These people will become your responsibility. And within you, our people will continue to grow and thrive," my father said to me. I could only wish to be as good of a king as him.

"Jabari," my mother whispered. "It is time."

My father smiled at me one last time before motioning for me to follow him. We were accompanied by members of the Canine Crew, Samael and his wives, and my future wife's parents. I was led deeper into the cavern that was poorly lit with torches and down some winding stairs.

We arrived at a hot spring where I was to be washed before my marriage. I didn't have on anything but a robe, and my new servant girls removed that. I stepped down into the steamy hot water and waited for the ladies to wash me.

As the girls ran their hands across my body with their soapy sponges, I could see that Agrat bat Mahlat was giving me the eye of desire. She watched me like a jealous lover. Samael could sense her want for me, but surprisingly, that did not faze him.

"If you want him, then indulge in his youth," he said to her. "I'm a man who doesn't mind sharing my wealth," he told me.

"This is not allowed," Na'amah snapped. "He is the forbidden fruit," she warned her.

"She is right. It is written in our laws that the elders cannot intermingle with the immortals," Lilith confirmed. "Although I would love to sample his sweet nectar myself," she smiled deceitfully.

When my body was cleaned, I stepped out of the water, exposing all of myself to the elder wives. My length and girth caused them to blush and giggle amongst themselves as the servant girls rushed to dress me in a white robe with golden trim.

I was then escorted into the ceremonial room, where my wife stood before the priest, awaiting my arrival. Her parents walked down the aisle as the Canine Crew surrounded the room. Samael and his wives were next, then my parents and myself.

This was the first time I was able to see the woman I was to marry. And as my father removed her veil, her beauty was undeniable. She was picture perfect, but something was pushing me away from her.

"You will love her in time," my mother whispered as she gave me a long and enduring hug.

"Her scent is off," I told her. "Something is not right with this one."

"Calm down, my son," my father whispered. "It's never right until you consummate the marriage."

I trusted my father, but I couldn't shake the feeling that she wasn't the one for me. With her parents approving of the ceremony, the priest began to pray over our union. From the Holy Well of Elohim, he dipped the Golden Goblet of Life in the water and filled it with the blessed water. He placed it into my hands to drink from it first. As I drank from the goblet, the water warmed my insides.

"These waters will grant you youth and health forever." The priest advised, then he took the goblet from my hand and gave it to my wife.

She drank from the goblet, but her reaction to the liquid was much different from mine. As she swallowed, I could see her chest spit fire as another tattoo was being etched into her skin. Lana pulled her robe open for all to see her new marking. It was located under her small, perky breasts, and it spanned the width of her chest. Her new tattoo was that of the Goddess Isis. This was a fertility blessing that she was awarded for becoming my wife.

I slightly glanced at Lilith, who was overjoyed, knowing that my first daughter would be her newest trophy.

My wife looked at me and smiled before saying, "I will give you many sons." Her voice was soft and calming, and her words were sincere. Maybe my father was right after all, although her scent was still off. Instead of pulling me to her, it was pushing me away.

After we traded our sacred vows, we were ushered to our new den, where we were to consummate our marriage. Our den was filled with viewers who were there to ensure that the deal was solidified.

She stood in front of me and removed her sheer robe, and announced, "Tonight, while the moon is high, I give my mind, body, and soul to you. Gethambe, you are my king; and I am your queen. I will fulfill all duties as your wife and will always be at your side for support. I will never degrade or question your authority. I will remain faithful, and I promise to give you sons to carry out your legacy," and then she bowed her head to me.

I reached over and lifted her head so that I could look into her soft, inviting eyes. When she smiled at me, I felt my heart warm, filled with a deep respect for her. I ran my finger down the side of her face, enjoying the softness of her skin against mine. I disrobed and pulled her close to my naked body.

I wanted to feel her skin against mine. I wanted to smell her gentle aroma. But standing next to her didn't allow me to extract the information I wanted from her. So, I kneeled in front of her, grabbed Lana by the hips, and pulled her pussy onto my face. My tongue flickered against her sweetness, trying to taste the juices that her sweet core had begun to leak generously. As my tongue darted in and out of her, licking and flicking her nub, I could feel a small attachment start to grow between us.

Her scent heightened, and my dick hardened with

want, my blood boiled with desire, as my eyes burned red in lust. As her juices flowed into my mouth, I growled and lapped it up eagerly, knowing that she was meant for me. This was the first woman I had ever tasted, and judging by her reaction, she was enjoying every moment of it.

I stood up, wiping her cream from my mouth, and looked at her. Not realizing my own strength, I picked her up and tossed her onto the bed. Then, I confidently demanded that she open herself to me. Without question, she leaned back onto the bed and spread her delectable, smooth legs wide, displaying her spirit to me.

I watched as she played with herself, her fingers toying with her clit, teasingly enticing me to join her. I grabbed my dick and began to stroke it slowly, and a rush of excitement ran through my spine. When I could not resist the temptation any longer, I pounced onto the bed and positioned myself between her legs.

Her scent engulfed my nostrils now. I gave an earth-shattering howl that was so powerful that it shook the mountains in the distance. With my dick thumping in anticipation, I pushed it into my wife in one quick stroke and began pounding into her without mercy. I felt her body try to resist me as I entered her, but it was no use. As I thumped into her, Lana grabbed my thick, muscular arms and dug her nails into my rough skin as she tried to pull away from me.

Without realizing my actions, I gripped her by the neck with one hand while using the other to pin her to the bed by her shoulder. As she began to howl from the intense pain that I was inflicting on her, I dipped my head into the crease of her neck and bit down sharply. Now, not only was she silent, but she was also incapacitated as I thrusted in and out of her wetness.

With each stroke, I delved deeper into her body, my dick trembling with depraved fury. I could feel that I was stretching Lana's pussy open, causing it to rip. But I couldn't stop. She would have to endure. I was on a quest for gratification, and unfortunately for her, she was the one chosen to help me get there.

Her quiet whining only excited me more, pushing me close to the edge. I quickened my stride, pumping into her as fast as I could. My heart pounded aggressively against my chest, and it became increasingly difficult for me to breathe. Each time I pushed into her, my hardness pulsed, its head becoming progressively sensitive with each stroke.

I felt my beast trying to emerge as I became over-whelmed with my new, increased sexual appetite. Before I morphed, I exploded, releasing my all into Lana, who laid still – cold and emotionless. I released her neck as my body bucked and jerked viciously.

I laid on top of her until the last of my seed dribbled from my dick. When I tried to pull out, Lana screamed out in pain. My dick was still swollen, and we were still stuck together, unable to separate.

"This is normal," my father explained. "Give yourself an hour or so for it to contract. Then you will be able to detach from one another."

I nodded my head, too tired to speak. Lana's pussy was still quivering around my delicate hardness, sending small waves of delight throughout my body.

Lana's mother approached her and began to stroke her hair as we lay in the bed, still locked together. I heard my wife panting and whimpering in displeasure under me.

"It's only hurtful the first couple of times," her mother whispered. "In time, your body will adapt, and your pain will turn into pleasure," she smiled.

Then Lilith approached the bed and slid her hand between our bodies to feel Lana's stomach. She smiled maliciously.

"Your seed was fertilized this night, but you will not see this child. I have already removed her from your womb."

I looked at my wife, who had tears streaming down her face. I understood her pain. We would never see this child, give her a name, or hold her in our arms. But this is the price to be paid for the many powers that had been bestowed upon our kind.

I licked her tears away and promised that she would become pregnant again. We had officially bonded. My beast accepted her beast, and together, we were the future of our pack.

As the room emptied and I was able to pull out of my wife, I noticed the pool of dark red blood that spilled from her sacred garden. Instead of calling upon the servant girls, I gathered the supplies and cleaned Lana myself.

Then I laid in the bed next to her and pulled her close to me. Together, we fell asleep as husband and wife.

LANA

Gethambe has been at it for weeks. Every night he comes into our chambers and pounds into me savagely. There is no compassion at all. I know that my job is to please him, but he is so brutal when sexing me.

I cry when I look at myself in the mirror. I don't even recognize the person staring back at me. My body is marked up with bite marks and scratches, I see bruises from his grip, and he is not in complete control of his wolf, so he keeps morphing into his beast. My body aches all the time, and he doesn't care. I cannot walk most mornings because my pussy throbs mercilessly from the constant savagery Gethambe inflicts.

I can't help but wonder when it's going to become more tolerable. And I wonder if my husband will ever make sweet, passionate love to me instead of ripping my sweetness to shreds. I want to be held and loved, nestled, and kissed, just treated as his wife instead of his whore. But then again, she may get more respect than I receive in the bedroom.

Today, I have to pull myself together and attend the Feast of Beast dinner with our families and friends. We celebrate our parents' departure into Edom with an elaborate meal with a variety of food. Most of the meats were hunted down and caught by the hunters, and the vegetables were grown here on our land. Although most of this is desert, the Gods make these grounds fertile to maintain our community.

For this reason, we are constantly in a fight with the mountain lions who have the ability to morph into human form as well. When their leader went against the Gods and made a pact with Lucifer, their lands were cursed. They cannot grow food or hunt there anymore. To care for themselves, they raid our land for its rich resources. We have tried many times to extend a helping hand to them, but they have become accustomed to being scavengers. They want everything or nothing at all.

Monthly, we lose at least one or two Canine Crew members to their attacks on our lands. But we have an advantage over them. Our soldiers are trained at an early age and then mentored in the field for several years before becoming a part of our security team. Another advantage is, they work in teams, moving as one unit. It is against our laws for a Canine Crew member to be alone, especially during these times.

"Are you going to lay around all day?" Gethambe asked as he walked into our chambers. His tone was so cold and heartless. Although we have bonded, I think he still has doubt in his heart about my commitment to him.

"No, My Love," I answered, pushing the thick buffalo blanket away from my body. "I'm getting up now to bathe and get ready," I explained.

"You and you," he elevated his voice while pointing to two of my chambermaids. "Help your mistress bathe and dress for dinner. I want to see her in something black, sleek, and pleasing to my eyes," he demanded.

"Yes, Sir," they replied in unison, gathering my things.

As I got out of bed, I whimpered in pain. It started from my feet and radiated up to my sweet spot. Every step was a challenge for me as I made my way to the hot springs.

"And the elders chose you to be my wife," he said sarcastically. "I can't even stick my dick in you without your ass whining like a pup."

"It's getting better, My Love," I tried to explain.

"Lana, if you can't satisfy me, I will replace your ass with someone who can," he snapped.

"Yes, My Love," I answered, crying on the inside. "I promise to be a better wife to you."

He looked at me in disgust and waved me away from him while he poured himself a drink. I made my way to the bath and stripped naked. I tried to place my hand on my vagina in hopes that I could heal myself, but I soon found out that my healing ability worked for everyone except me. So, I stepped into the water and prayed that the warmth would soothe my aches and pains.

"My Lady," one of my chambermaids said. "My mother is a doctor and has mixed these herbs for your pain. She did the same for the past queen when she first married the past king." Then she laid the small glass jar on the concrete ground by the bathing hole.

"And how do I use this cream?" I asked.

"Just rub it on any sore area of your body, and it will numb the pain," she directed.

"After each encounter?" I needed to know.

"Yes, My Lady. But I would apply it after this bath so that your body can start to heal before the king revisits your bed," she replied with her head lowered to the floor.

"And why do you ladies always walk around here with your head down? Seeing you do that depresses me," I snapped.

"Because you are royalty, My Lady. We have no right to look at you," she responded quietly.

"Well, that changes today. Just because you are my chambermaid doesn't mean that you are not a thriving and productive member of this society. As of today, you will bow as we walk past you, but after you show your respect, you will hold your head up as high as I hold mine," I told her.

I saw their faces glow with the news and one of them smiled slightly at me. It made my heart fill with joy to add pleasure to someone else's life.

I washed my body and applied the cream given to me as a gift to help my body accept my husband without me yelling out in excruciating pain. Maybe tonight, I would even surprise him and initiate the mating process. Be more like the humans and make it meaningful to him.

After getting dressed in something that my husband felt

was fitting for tonight, I walked to the dining hall. As I walked down the hall, up the winding stairs, and to my destination, I felt no pain. The cream worked instantly.

"Now, you look like a queen," Gethambe said to me.

His eyes were filled with desire as he stared at me hungrily. When I went to take my place at his side, I saw him lick his lips with want. This is what I wanted from him, the reaction that my heart longed for.

My dress was long and form-fitting. It was black as he requested but all lace. I wore no panties or bra, but the lacy design concealed my jewels from prying eyes. But what made the dress the most appealing were the diamonds that were embroidered in it that sparkled under the soft dim light of the torches.

I waited for my husband to sit before I took my seat. Before the great feast, the family had to discuss old business. Gethambe will not only be the Alpha Male of our pack, but he would be in control of the casino that our people own in town, the cleaning business, and the two hotels.

"You need to make your presence known at the casino. That is our biggest investment," Jabari said to Gethambe. "They already know that my son is taking over the family business."

"What needs to be done?" Gethambe asked him.

"Everything. Thousands of dollars are exchanged in there daily. You have to double-check everyone. Man can't be trusted," he warned.

"And what about the other businesses?" Gethambe asked.

"First of all, you need to appoint two or three trust-worthy men to help you with managing the daily operations of the casino. That is our lifeline to financial stability. Although we hunt for our meat and grow our vegetables, money is how we care for the pack. And keep in mind that everyone has a job here. Nobody stays within this society without contributing something."

My husband looked puzzled. I don't think he knew that he had to take on so much responsibility. But his will to survive will help him through this rough patch.

"My Love," I said, placing my hand on his. "May I make a suggestion?"

"What is it, Lana? Men are talking," he snapped. I knew that I wasn't supposed to interfere, but I felt that my input was valuable.

"You are close to your cousins Darwin and Joseph; maybe they would be suitable to help you manage the busi-nesses," I suggested, in a delightful and low voice.

Before I could finish my words, I felt a stinging sensa-tion across my face. Everyone was looking as Gethambe slapped me. I dare not ask what I had done wrong, but I knew that I was about to find out.

"Know your place, woman. You have no voice when it comes to business. The only voice you have is when I'm ramming my dick deep into your pussy," he said, his voice slightly elevated.

"Yes, My Love," I apologized, trying not to show that I was embarrassed at being treated like shit for trying to be helpful.

"Give me some space. Go to your den until I call for you," he directed.

A punishment, I thought to myself as I stood up and walked away from the table. What have I done to make him hate me so?

I was only trying to help. I knew how close he was to his cousins because they were raised together as pups. Although they had no claim to the crown, they were his family – people I knew he trusted with his life.

I went to our den and sat on the bed. I asked the chambermaids to leave because I needed a little time to myself. I needed to think about how I was going to redeem my actions. However, I didn't have much time to myself because within minutes, Ebonee and my mother, Cherish, were coming through the door.

As they walked through the door, they both gave me a concerned look that made my skin crawl with insecurities.

"Lana, what is going on between you and Gethambe?" Ebonee asked.

"And why would you interrupt the men while they were discussing business?" My mother questioned.

"Gethambe doesn't want me. I don't understand what it is that I'm doing wrong," I said with tears cascading down my face. "And when we mate, I am unable to handle him, especially when his beast is fighting so hard to emerge," I explained. "And as far as me getting into their business, I was only offering a suggestion. Isn't that what queens do?"

"Lana," my mother said with pity dancing in her voice. "You know the tradition of our people and the role that you play in it. Because this marriage was arranged before you were born, you received all the training and schooling you needed to prepare you for this moment. It's not your place to offer suggestions, at least not at the table with the men. In privacy behind closed doors is when you whisper ideas to your husband."

"Dear sweet child," Ebonee said. "I told you that sex would not be easy with him. I have endured it for years. They are strong men with a vigorous appetite. But if you practice relaxing your body as he enters you, it will go so much smoother. With time, you will adjust to his needs and be able to manage the situation better."

"With time...with time...everything is *'with time'*!" I said, slightly raising my voice. "I want the fairytale ending now. I want my husband to make love to me and treat me like the queen I am. Not like his whore."

"Lana!" my mother yelled. "Hush your mouth and respect your Elder Queen," she stated, slapping me across my face.

In all my years, my mother has never struck me. For her to slap me, I knew I had to be wrong and totally disrespectful.

"I apologize," I said to Ebonee. "I was out of line with my words and tone. Please forgive me."

"Apology accepted. But you need to pull yourself together before you piss him and me off. I'm only trying to help you, Lana. Not hurt you," she explained. "Now clean your face, and let's go have dinner. Gethambe is expecting you to return with us. I'm only going to say this once; sit beside your husband, look pretty, but shut the hell up."

I got up and cleaned my face, wiping away all the

hurt and pain of this life. Then, gracefully, I entered the hall with Queen Ebonee and my mother, taking my seat at the head of the table beside my husband. Although I could feel my husband's eyes burning through me, I maintained a smile on my face. Even as he growled at my presence, I remained refined and quiet. He knew that his mother had been consoling me, which made me weak in his eyes.

After dinner, I gave Gethambe his space to say his goodbyes to his parents while I said goodbye to mine. It was my job as the new queen to escort them to Edom. The journey will require me to be away from my husband and the den for a couple of days. This would give my body time to heal and the space we needed to clear our heads.

We all walked together to the portal room, and Gethambe touched his necklace and chanted a few words. A door appeared into the cavern wall. When I opened it, I could feel the tranquility of Edom welcoming me. The feeling made me wish I was going there to stay with my parents as well. But that was impossible; I was a married woman now and the Alpha Female of our pack. My title required me to stay here on this ratchet earth until the next king was born and took the crown. And that could take a thousand years or more.

I walked over to my husband and kissed him on his cheek. "I will be home soon," I said to him.

"No rush," he answered. "Take your time and make sure your parents settle into their new life. And make sure my parents settle into theirs," he said. His reasoning may have sounded good, but it wasn't heartfelt. He didn't care if

I came home to him or not. I believe that he was hoping I died during the transition from Earth to Edom.

"Quit being silly," I tried to joke with him. "I can't wait to come back home to you. We have some catching up to do. I believe I'm ready to accept all of you, My Love," I whispered in his ear.

If nothing else, that bought out the twinkle in his eyes and a smile on his face. So much so that he wrapped his arms around my waist and pulled me close to him. He looked at me, staring deep into my soul, trying to figure out if I was being honest about what I was saying.

"You think you can handle me now because you had a chit-chat with my mother?" he smiled.

"I know I can handle you now," I answered.

"This we shall see," he laughed. "I kind of like it when you fight back and resist."

"Well, I guess now you're going to have to get used to your wife enjoying every minute with you," I smiled at him as I planted several soft kisses on his luscious lips.

Gethambe returned the affection, kissing me softly as he sucked on my bottom lip. His hand caressed my ass, squeezing it in front of our families. He felt so good that I didn't want to let him go. But I had to.

"In that case, hurry back to me. I love a challenge," he joked. "Next time, I'm really going to split that ass in half, and I better not hear you whimper or whine. All I want to hear are moans of ecstasy and pleasure," he demanded.

"And you will, My Love." I guaranteed. I felt that I was true to my word because if he did rip my pussy apart, I had that cream to mend it back together. I was ready for him and all he thought he could do to me. Besides, I figured that this was the wedge between us, and if I could do this one simple thing, I would receive the love and acceptance that I so desperately wanted from him.

As I pulled away from his arms, he held his nose high in the air and began sniffing it. "What is that smell?" he asked, with excitement in his voice.

We all raised our heads and began to sniff, but I didn't smell anything, and neither did my mother or Ebonee. But my father and Jabari caught a whiff of it. And whatever it was, it had all of their attention.

"Whatever it is, it will subside. But we must get moving," I announced. Once the Portal of Life has been opened, I only have a small amount of time to get them to the other side.

Ebonee and my mother stepped through the portal together and waited for their husbands, who were still sniffing the air. So, I pulled my father by his hand and pushed Jabari into the portal. It was only then that they were able to focus.

Before the portal closed, Jabari said, "Be careful of that, son. That smells too good to be true."

Then the portal closed before I could find out what the hell was going on. It would have to wait until we arrive in Edom. There I could ask my father about the strange aroma in the air that only the men could smell.

7

ASHLEY

I had to make a trip back to Jacksonville because my mother had passed away. I feel guilty that I didn't move her here with me. But with her dementia, I thought it was best to leave her in the upscale nursing facility where she had become adjusted to the staff and her surroundings.

Now, here I am, back in the one place I didn't want to be making funeral arrangements for my mother. And to make it worse, she died on Mother's Day. This holiday will always bring sadness to my life, even when I have children of my own.

I had to stop by the nursing facility first to handle my financial responsibility. While there, they asked me what I wanted to do with her belongings. I would donate most of the furnishings along with her clothes, but I knew she kept a picture album that meant a lot to me. It was filled with memories of the early years of my life, pictures of my father, and news clippings of family members that had passed.

Once I handled all my mother's affairs, my body was

exhausted, and I was overwhelmed. I figured that I would have a nice, quiet meal accompanied by a couple of drinks to calm my nerves. I wanted to be left alone as I reminisced over better days.

The one place I felt comfortable and relaxed was Ruth's Chris Steakhouse. Not only was their food good, but the atmosphere was inviting, and they had an amazing view of the St. Johns River. I loved to just sit by the large glass windows, look out onto the city, and sip on a glass of wine. At night, the scenery was absolutely gorgeous. That is the only time I really enjoyed the continuous energy of the city life.

As soon as I arrived there, it was like old times. I was welcomed in without even having a reservation and given my old table. Although I was feeling down and out, I began to feel a little better. The atmosphere of Ruth's Chris was warm and sensual and gave me a sense of tranquility.

"It's been a long time," the greeter said to me.

"I don't live here anymore," I answered, following him to my table.

"And where did the lady move to?" he asked, pulling my chair out for me.

"Winslow, Arizona," I replied.

"Get prepared for the heat," he grinned. "And will your husband be joining you today?"

"Not this time. We are divorced," I explained, clearing my throat.

"My apologies," he said. "Antinori Tignanello, tonight?" he questioned. I was impressed that he remembered that. It was one of my favorite wines.

I smiled at him graciously and answered, "That would be nice. I haven't had a glass in a while. The area I moved to doesn't have the luxury of such a fine wine. Or should I say I haven't found an establishment that offers it?"

He nodded his head and walked away, leaving me to my thoughts and deep in my emotions. I looked out the window and watched the cars as they crossed the bridge, the tour boats gliding along the river, and the young lovers walking along the boardwalk. Seeing the couples holding hands and hugging made me realize exactly how lonely I was. They had everything I craved.

As my wine arrived, the waiter asked me if I was ready to order. I wasn't hungry, so I asked him to check on me later. I just wanted to enjoy the soft music playing in the background, watch the sunset, and think about all the good times I shared with my mother before she got sick.

He didn't ask any other questions; he just nodded his head in acceptance and left me to enjoy my peaceful evening. But peace doesn't last forever.

"Ashley," I heard a familiar voice say.

I turned my head and looked up to find William staring down at me. "William," I replied sarcastically.

"Wow," he said. "I almost forgot how beautiful you are."

"Cut the bullshit, William. What do you want?" I snapped. Just hearing his voice made me sick to my stomach. I turned my head to look out of the window as I took a sip of wine.

"I heard about your mother," he answered. "I know how close you were to her, and I can't imagine the pain that you're going through." Then he pulled out the chair across the table from me.

I looked at him in disgust and said with an evil tone, "I didn't invite you to have a seat."

"I know. I know. But it looked like you needed a little company. Nobody should have to deal with what you're dealing with alone. Let's just be friends – just for this evening," he pleaded, smiling at me. He had a way of making me melt in his arms. "We loved each other at one point. Besides, we have a lot of history together; not every memory you have of me is bad," he said. His grin was chipping a little anger away at a time.

"Like you were there for me when I had a miscarriage with our child?" Yet, as much as I hated this man, I was still deeply in love with him. *Why?* I thought to myself.

"Look, Ashley. I admit I was wrong for the things I did, but you were no angel. Hell, maybe if you respected me as a man and allowed me to be the head of the house, things probably would have been a lot different. But your problem was, you couldn't. You had to be in control of everything, all the fucking time. And you thought that since you had money, it would make me stay, so you took joy in rubbing my nose in your success and my failures. Fuck – I loved you. But sometimes a person just has to know when to walk away from a situation before it becomes a devastation," he said in a low tone whisper. His words were sharp and cut me to my core.

"But I never cheated on you, William," I replied sarcastically. "I was always there when you needed me. But when I needed you, you were laid between that bitch's legs. So, miss me with that petty ass bullshit you're spitting. Grab a fucking tissue for your issues because I don't give a damn about them anymore," I said, sipping from my glass again.

"Look, we can sit here all evening and throw punches back and forth, but I'd rather just be a shoulder to cry on. Your mother just passed away, you don't have any real friends, and you cut off your entire family from what I hear. So, let me be here for you, if only for a couple of hours," he implored.

"Whatever," I told him. "Make yourself comfortable, interrupting my quiet little evening," I said. To be honest, I was thrilled to see him, and it was nice to have someone to talk to. I just loved him so much that I hated him. "Order whatever you want. I have to go to the ladies' room; I'll be right back. *If* you're still here when I return, I will be respectful enough to put our differences aside and have dinner with you."

"I will be here," he laughed.

I looked at him with my perfect bitch face, cutting my eyes and twisting my lips. "Whatever," I hissed, getting up from the table.

I made my way to the ladies' room thinking about William. Why? I don't know. Maybe it was because I was an emotional wreck, or perhaps it was that I loved the way he made me feel. He knew exactly what to say and how to say the things I wanted to hear. It's a shame our marriage didn't survive.

After handling my business, I walked to the sink and washed my hands. As I looked into the mirror, I realized I needed to freshen up. My makeup had worn off, and I looked tired and defeated. I looked at the woman in the mirror and laughed quietly, thinking about what my mother would have said if she had seen me like this. It was only because of her that I was so constantly concerned with my appearance. My mother was a very vain woman who never went anywhere without putting on her best face. The funny thing was that my grandmother was the complete opposite – I remembered her preaching to us that *'only clowns wore face paint.'*

I reached into my purse to grab my face powder when I noticed William coming through the door. By the time he had stepped through the door and locked it, he had my total undivided attention.

"What are you doing?" I laughed.

"What do you think," he answered, removing his tie and unbuttoning his shirt.

"William...no," I said sternly.

He approached me as he threw his shirt onto the floor and unbuttoned his pants. We may not have gotten along in recent times, and our divorce was bitter till the end, but my lady missed him. William had an extremely large package that sent me to the moon and beyond *repeatedly*. I couldn't get enough of it. When I first found out about the other woman in his life, I was jealous as hell because I knew he was giving it to her the way he used to give it to me.

"William...I said no," I repeated, looking at him through the mirror.

Ignoring me, I saw him massaging his dick in his hand, priming it for action. He stood close to me, and I felt it throb as he rubbed it against my ass. The slightest touch made my clit pulse with want.

"Please...don't," I whispered, leaning onto the sink.

I was too weak and emotionally vulnerable to put up a viable resistance to the temptation of his offer. I hated to admit it, by my body missed the masculinity of a real man.

He was so close to me that I could feel his breath tickle the back of my neck. It was warm and stimulating, exciting every nerve in my body.

"You really want me to stop?" he whispered in my ear as he nibbled on it, wrapping his arms around my waist.

God knows I didn't need this shit right now, but my body was calling for him.

"Y-yes," I moaned, leaning my head backward onto his shoulder, my body behaving very differently from how I wanted it to.

I closed my eyes and enjoyed the sensual kisses that he began to rain down my neck as he dry-humped my ass. My body was fully relaxed, and I felt myself start to warm between the legs with excited passion.

I felt his hand slowly trickle down the contours of my body, pulling my skirt up as it searched fervently for its final, prized destination. When he had my skirt pulled up to my waist, he slid his fingers into my panties, down my valley, and in between my tight, locked lips. When he found my hidden pearl, he began to jiggle his finger against it softly, with just the right amount of pressure.

"*Mmmmh*," I moaned fervently, indulging in this forbidden dance of seduction.

"Still want me to stop?" he asked while sucking on my neck.

With every movement he made with his skilled finger, I could feel small waves of ecstasy racing throughout my body. Every time he kissed or sucked on my neck, I felt like prey in the grasp of its robust and dominant predator.

"No," I whispered.

Then, he pulled his hand from my panties and pulled them down just below my ass. He used one hand to push me forward and his foot to kick my legs apart. William slid his hardness up and down my ass teasing me before he thrust it into the opening of my sweetness. And I enjoyed every second of it.

His thick, hard dick filled my entire pussy to the hilt, and I felt myself wrap snugly around him. The sensation of feeling the length of his thick, heated shaft buried deep inside me was simply breathtaking. I felt myself beginning to cream all over him.

He chuckled, knowing the effect he had on me, as he pulled me back onto him.

"Can't no man do for you what I can," he said.

And as of today, he was right. Only he was able to make my body explode simply upon entrance.

William began to push into me slowly as I moved back onto him. His hands dug firmly into my hips as his dick thumped with anticipation, and his low groans grew louder.

When he increased his pace, I felt my body quiver with excited eagerness, my heart pound with lust, and my breathing was labored with desire. I was falling fast into a sweet euphoric release, and I was willing to let myself go.

"Faster – Harder – More!" I screamed, moaning.

I must have been too loud because he leaned forward and used one hand to cover my mouth while holding me tightly by my waist with the other.

I looked into the mirror and saw that his eyes were closed and that he was biting down on his bottom lip as he fucked me hard and fast. He slid in and out of my wetness with solid and precise strokes.

The heat from his body and the sweat that dribbled down his face excited me. He was pounding fiercely into me, and the sound of our skin slapping filled the entire bathroom. The steam we created gave off the strong, musky aroma of his cologne, mixed with our heated, debauched lust.

My sensitive nub was throbbing, my blood was boiling, and my body was quivering as my cream streamed out of me and onto his long, thick rod. He felt so good inside me that tears began to swell in my eyes. I couldn't resist indulging myself anymore. I wanted to be satisfied.

William slammed into me with a powerful thrust and shot his nectar into my core. His body bucked and jerked with every squirt, and he groaned as he emptied his manhood of his seed deep inside of me. Releasing his grip on my mouth, he stood there, still inside me, out of breath and too weak to speak.

I looked into the mirror and watched him. I could feel as his dick pulsated in me while it released the last drops of his sweet love.

"I miss you," I said, smiling like a teenage girl. "I miss this."

"Yeah, Baby. I do too," he huffed, pulling himself out of me.

I grabbed a couple of tissues and cleaned myself up. William did the same.

"You want to come back to the hotel with me tonight?" I asked him, still captivated by the moment. "I'll make it worth your while," I smiled seductively, pulling up my panties and re-adjusting my skirt.

He looked at me, and I could see the conflict in his eyes. Immediately, my desire for him evaporated. My heart knew what he was about to say.

"I...I have to go home to my girl," he answered.

I turned to William and slapped him so hard that his cheek reddened, and an imprint of my hand formed on it.

"I knew better. I fucking knew better," I snapped. "I don't even know why I keep falling for your bullshit."

"Ashley, you know I have a woman at home. I didn't lie to you about my situation," he said, teetering toward anger. "I wanted to do this because I had not been able to satisfy her at home. I just wanted to make sure it still worked, and evidently, it does."

"Then if Mrs. Right is at home waiting for you, why are you here in this bathroom fucking me?" I asked, tears now streaming down my face as I swung my fist at him wildly.

He caught my arm quickly.

"I saw you. I wanted you. And I knew you would give it to me," he said simply.

Somehow, he had managed to piss me off even more.

"Just get your shit and get out!" I yelled. "I don't want to ever see your face again, William. Even if you see me walking down the street, don't fucking come near me," I told him, sobbing hysterically.

He gathered his things and redressed himself. He looked at me, shaking his head as if I should have known what this was about. I knew I shouldn't have done this to myself, but he caught me at an emotional, weak moment and used that to his advantage.

When he finished dressing, he kissed me on my cheek and said, "Believe it or not, I will always love you, but for my sanity and yours, we just can't go down that road again."

"But it's okay that you fucked me?"

He looked at me and turned to walk away. As he unlocked the door, he asked if it would be okay to attend my mother's funeral.

"There won't be a funeral. She is being cremated at her request. Now get the fuck out of my face!"

William shook his head in disbelief and walked out of the door. I ran into a bathroom stall and allowed all my emotions to run out of me like water. I cried, and cried, and cried until I had no more tears left in my body. I cried because of my divorce; I cried because I lost my father, and I cried a river because I lost my mother. I was officially alone. I had money, but I lacked family and friends. And the one man I loved was in love with someone else. I felt like my life was heading in a downward spiral.

8

GETHAMBE

"What the fuck!" I yelled out, waking up.

I have been plagued by this aroma that has been filling the air for a couple of days. The first night I smelled it, my dick hardened with want. An hour or two later, the scent died down. But whatever it is, it's back, and the aroma is so strong that I cannot sleep.

"Sir," the chambermaid said. "Are you okay?"

"Do I look okay?" I snapped. My eyes were red as fire, I'm cranky as hell, and here lately, I always look like I have a hangover. Not to mention that when the smell is at its strongest, my dick is hard as steel, and nothing relieves it.

"No, Sir," she answered. "You look tired." After answering, she stood there and waited for a response.

"I am fucking tired, and my dick aches for pleasure," I yelled at her.

She didn't say a word but immediately began to disrobe. I looked at her and wasn't the least bit aroused. She was too skinny, too pale, and too used up by my father for me to be attracted to her.

"I can help you with that," she finally spoke.

"If my wife can't handle me, what in the hell makes you think you can?" my tone was harsh. "Put your clothes on, child, and find me a piece of suitable pussy for me to fuck," I demanded. "I like a thick woman who is older but less experienced than you."

She picked up her belongings from the floor and hurried away. As soon as I had a free moment, I would replace all the chambermaids with some ladies who hadn't been used up. I love my father, but I'm not that one for sloppy seconds. I would never allow my dick to mingle with any of the bitches he fucked. Besides, my taste in women was totally different from his. Jabari liked those unhealthy-looking chicks, looking like he had deprived them of food for a couple of months. I wanted a woman with some meat on her bones, not too much meat, but enough to grab when I'm digging deep into her.

Lana wasn't bad and would be a lot better if she could handle the dick. I'm still not vibing with her scent, but she's my wife, and we are mated for life. It almost makes me hate traditions. Why couldn't I pick someone that I fell in love with instead of them telling me who I could love? Lana is a beautiful woman, but I can feel it in every bone in my body that I don't love her. But to get my rocks off, I'll fuck the shit out of that bitch. One thing about her, I love to hear her scream because that shit makes me cum hard as fuck!

"FUUUCCKKK!" I yelled out as my dick stiffened. That aroma was driving me insane with lust. I needed to have one of these women to help take care of my problem before I fucked around and got blue balls.

I heard the footsteps of the chambermaid and turned to look toward the door. She was exactly what the doctor ordered. She was tall, dark-skinned, and voluptuous. Her walk was elegant and seductive, and those baby-blue eyes yanked my heart right out of my chest. And what pulled me into her essence was that she smelled pleasing but not perfect. I could fuck her without becoming nauseated like I sometimes became with Lana.

She bowed her head as she walked through the doorway and held her arms out with her palms up. She was showcasing her body, and I was enjoying the view. Her breasts were full and appetizing, her hips were thick, and her ass was firm, sitting high.

"You called for me, My Lord?" she questioned.

"Remove your clothes and get into bed," I demanded.

"With the utmost respect, My Lord, but when the king takes a mistress, he usually takes her in the harlot's chamber, not in the bed that he shares with his queen," she informed me meekly, her eyes to the ground.

"And where might that be?" I inquired.

My father never told me about a chamber to fuck my whores in – which reminded me I needed to ask this bitch if my father had ever fucked her.

"Before we get started, I need to know if you have ever slept with my father."

"I will show you the chamber, follow me," she directed. "To answer your second question, no, My Lord, I have never had the pleasure of sleeping with the Elder King. He didn't take too kindly to women who were as heavy as me," she explained in a sweet and delicate voice.

I followed the servant girl through the dark hallway and down a spiral flight of stairs. We walked through a second dark hallway and arrived at a large, heavy door. This must be the entrance to the room I was expected to use when mingling with the ladies of pleasure. She opened the door, stepped inside, and politely waited at the doorway for me to enter the room behind her. Then, she closed the door and ushered me to the bed.

"Look, I don't have the time or energy for all that lovey, dovey shit. I don't want to marry you; I just want to fuck you. So, disrobe and lie down," I commanded.

She nodded her head and did as she was told. After she lay in bed, spreading her legs open for me, I stripped out of my pajamas and made my way over to her. I crawled up to her from the foot of the bed and rubbed my nose in her pussy. Disappointingly, her scent was annoyingly foul but more bearable than Lana's.

I climbed up to her and laid my body on top of hers, the length of my shaft resting against her stomach. The pressure gave me some relief from the constant aching of my incessant, everlasting erection.

When the pain subsided, I reached down and grabbed my manhood in my hand and rubbed its head teasingly against the length of her pussy and her small, wet clit. As she became moist with desperate want, I slowly pushed my head into her tight opening. I was surprised – she was tight for a chambermaid, and it felt like a fight to the finish as I struggled to fit the girth of my thick, swollen hardness into her.

She squirmed and yelped, trying to push away from me, but I forcefully pushed deeper into her pussy. Her tensed tightness strangled my dick, but it only enticed me to push as much of myself into her as I possibly could.

I could see the pain was killing her, and she whimpered like a wounded pup. As I fully submerged myself into her wetness, she again desperately tried to push me off her and begged for mercy.

"Are you a fucking virgin?" I asked her, irritated by her resistance but still holding off the urge to cum as her pussy tightened around my cock like a vice.

"No," she cried. "But you're enormous... and it hurts so bad."

I almost felt bad for the servant whore, but I needed to bust one, nonetheless. Judging by how tight she was, it wasn't going to take me long at all.

"Just lay here and be still for a minute. I need to calm myself, or I'll rip you little pussy to shreds," I warned her. The chase was the most exciting part about sex for me.

Heeding my warning, she lay as still as she could aside from her deep, labored breaths. I tried to control myself, but as I watched her chest heave, her breasts dancing and jiggling under the candlelight, my dick swelled even more, pulsing with lust.

Without realizing it, I begin to pound into my servant girl viciously. I was deaf to her cries and blinded to her tears as elation ran rampantly through my veins. My body was on fire, my balls were tight, my breathing was heavy, and my heart was pounding fiercely against my chest.

I thrusted into her with an uncontrollable fury, but, as good as she felt, I was not able to cum. The harder I slammed into her, the louder she howled. The deeper I dove, the more she resisted me. My dick swelled, pulsed, and shuddered as I hammered into her, but mystifyingly, I couldn't get any release from this aching pain in my dick. I couldn't cum, and it was driving me crazy.

Without warning, I evolved into my beast. Half-man and half-wolf, pounding into her with the power of the Gods. Thankfully, she was wet, tight, and warm – all the things I loved about women, and in my beastly state, I could enjoy these beautiful qualities of hers with a heightened sensitivity.

As the aroma blew away with the wind, so did my drive to cum. I slowed my pace until I was able to catch my breath and come to my senses. I knew that I had to morph back into my human form.

I looked down onto the maiden, who was terrified of my sexual rage.

"As soon as my hardness subsides, I will let you go," I promised, with a tinge of remorse in my voice.

"Yes, My Lord," she answered. Her voice was trembling, and her body quivered slightly beneath mine.

It took half an hour of us being locked in an awkward embrace before I was able to pull out of her. I lifted my body and sat on the side of the bed. She hurriedly hopped out of bed and ran to her robe that was lying on the floor. She wrapped it around her body and stood in front of me, waiting for permission to be dismissed.

"Leave," I told her. "But I may call on you again. Next time make sure you are prepared for me," I said to her; my voice was cold and stern.

"Yes, My Lord," she replied.

She bowed her head and ran to the door, escaping my gaze as quickly as she could.

I sat on the side of the bed and thought about the strange aroma and the size of my dick. Both of them were causing some significant issues in my life at this point. My wife acts as if I am ripping her apart whenever I get the opportunity to sex her, and now the chambermaid is terrified of my dick.

But what puzzles me more is the strange smell that has repeatedly stimulated my dick. It is pushing my hormones into overdrive. I couldn't even sleep when the wind blew that scent just right and carried it into my chambers. That smell is like dick crack, seriously.

The only way to find out what it is and where it is coming from is to follow the scent to its originator. I have to know who she is and why she is insisting on tormenting me so.

So, I sprang from my bed and dressed quickly. I raced up to my den and had the chambermaid tell four of my top Canine Crew members to meet me at the entrance to our secret society. I told her to advise them to be prepared to fight, just in-case this was a setup. I didn't want to lose my life because of some tantalizing aroma that I knew nothing about.

I cleaned myself up quickly and made my way to the

golden gates that allowed you to leave and enter our compound. I gave the signal to the gatekeeper to lower our cloaking shield and open the gates. Then, we transformed into our wolves, and my pack followed me as I led them through the desert. We were running at top speed with my nose in the air, following the scent that was driving my hormones crazy.

As I reached the place where the smell was the strongest, I was shocked to see that it was coming from a humanoid home. I have roamed these lands for years and have never come across this building. So, whoever lives there, just had this place built.

"Rouge," I said telepathically. "Go check it out. But stay out of sight."

He nodded his head and slowly walked over to the house. As he started to round the building, he disappeared into the night.

We stood there for several minutes when the wind blew in our direction, causing us all to howl. My crew was picking up her scent, and I was bathing in it. Her smell caused me to involuntarily morph back into human form. There I stood, in front of my soldiers, with my dick growing in length and swelling in girth.

"FUUUCCCKK!" I yelled out. "This shit hurts," I continued.

With all eyes on me and my reaction to the aroma that engulfed us, my pack began to howl out of control. I could even hear Rogue howling from the back of the house. As I dealt with the stretching of my manhood, I could hear the pack talking in my head. They were confused and curious as much as I was.

"Why are you in human form?" Juice questioned.

"What is that smell?" Stewart inquired.

"Fuck all that. Why is this nigga's dick bigger than mine?" Joker giggled.

As much as I wanted to laugh at Joker, I was at the tip of a severe anxiety attack. If I couldn't get a grasp on this shit and quick, I was going to fuck around and have a heart attack. All because I couldn't get the pussy I craved. Ain't that some shit for you?

As the smell dissipated, my hardness relaxed. At the same time, Rouge was approaching with his report.

He looked at me suspiciously and said, "It's a human girl, and she just finished bathing."

"Could you smell any type of beast in her?" I wanted to know, shifting back into my wolf.

"None that I could tell. All I could smell was the blood of a woman and a faint scent of a man," Rouge stated.

"Did you see a man in the house?" I wanted to know. For a taste of that sweet shit, I would kill a motherfucker.

"I walked around the house and peeked through every window, but I didn't see a human male," he answered.

I needed to see her for myself. I wanted to know who she was and what she looked like. Usually, our kind isn't attracted to women outside our species, but something about her pulled me into her being.

"I don't think you should get close," Rouge said, concerned that her scent might make me transform again.

"Yeah, Gethambe, I don't think you're thinking with the right head," Joker joked.

I looked at him and sneered, showing my pearly, white, long canines. As I growled and flexed, Joker backed down, realizing that I was no longer in the playing mood.

I have known Rouge, Joker, Stewart, and Juice my whole life. We played together as pups and grew together as boys until they were taken to join the Canine Crew. But even after that, we remained extremely close. So much so that I knew, without a doubt in my mind, that any one of them would lay down their lives to protect mine. Not only were they the best of the best, but they were fiercely loyal to my family and me. It's just right now; I don't want to play and hang out like old friends. I want to find out how this witch was casting such a spell on me. She had to be conspiring with one of the archangels or perhaps Lucifer himself. Lucifer's demons and Demi-Gods were always after us. Because we were the protectors of First Heaven, we were constantly in a battle with his realm.

I looked at Rouge, signaling him to take a walk with me. I told Juice, Joker, and Stewart to keep low and stay out of sight. I wasn't really worried that they would be seen because we were under the cover of darkness, and we were far enough from the street to where any passing cars couldn't see us.

Rouge led the way as I followed close behind him. As we approached the house, I could hear a piano playing some soft jazz music. I peered into the large bay window in the front of the house, and there she sat, in front of a fireplace, reading a book and drinking wine from a flute-style glass.

She was absolutely gorgeous. Her skin was mocha and smooth, her face young and angelic, and her frame was small and very feminine. I inhaled the air and fell deeply in love with her. The aroma her body released flowed through me like a steady stream and aroused every drop of blood in my body. She was sent from the Heavens for my delight. The Gods had made this flawless creature for me.

I was lost in thought when I heard Rouge's voice ground me back down to reality.

"We need to go. You had your chance to see her; now we need to go," he warned.

But I didn't want to leave her. I wanted to watch her all night long and into the morning. I didn't want to go back to the den and spend the rest of my life with Lana. I wanted to be right here, with her.

"King Gethambe," Rouge said, his voice elevating slightly inside of my head.

"WHAT!" I yelled back at him.

He lowered his head, giving me my respect before saying, "Sir. We can't stay here. It's not safe for you. This house is on the border of our land and the forbidden desert."

I looked around to survey our surroundings. And to my disappointment, he was right. This wasn't a good place for me to be, and I had been out too long. As much as I wanted to stay and gaze upon this magnificent creature, I had to go.

I took one final look at her as she gracefully picked up the glass and sipped from it. I loved the way she wrapped her lips around the rim of her glass and allowed the wine to slide into her mouth. When she laid it back down onto the table, I noticed that she wiggled her toes slightly. Even that turned me on.

Then I turned and made my way back to Juice, Joker, and Stewart, who was waiting for us behind a small hill. We then made our way back to the den. The whole run home, I thought of only her. And anyone who had the shape-shifting ability knew it, including Lana.

It has been lovely spending time with my family and getting them settled into Edom. It was a beautiful place to live out eternity. It was built like the old world on Earth. All the buildings were constructed with baked mud bricks and stone. Huge trees lined the stone-paved roads, and the people here used horses and carriages to get around. Everything here was clean, fresh, and inviting. No matter where you went, your body was overcome with a sense of serenity.

I finally met the young girl who gave herself to my husband as a sacrifice. It was my job to ensure that her family had prominent positions and that she wanted for nothing. Because she gave her life for my husband to have two, she was treated like royalty. She stayed in a gorgeous palace with all the other girls from past sacrifices. They had servant girls and luxury furnishings. None of them wanted for anything because everything was given to them.

These young girls would marry in time, but only to a man the Gods felt was suitable. He had to be a noble, like them, unmarried, and pure of heart. Although they were not virgins, they were considered one because of the way their virginity was lost. So, they were entitled to be treated with the utmost respect.

Since being here, my soul has not rested. Something back home wasn't quite right. Before entering the portal of life, something caught the attention of my husband, my father, and the Elder King, Jabari. And the way Jabari told Gethambe to be careful sent chills racing throughout my body.

Today I was meeting with Samael; he invited me to his quarters for dinner and to talk about my marriage. Although the elders knew there was a mountain of problems between my husband and me, they wanted to hear it from my mouth with their own ears. It scares me to talk about this with them because if this union doesn't work, and they feel that Gethambe needs a stronger mate, I will be recycled. Because I was a queen of our pack, I would be allowed to enter the reincarnation cycle and be reborn to repeat life. I would be born into another pack in another realm, as another future queen.

"Daddy," I said. "I am worried about my future," I confided in him as I fixed breakfast.

"Have patience with him," my mother intervened, walking gracefully into the kitchen.

"I am being patient. I am submissive, attentive, and loyal. His wish is my command. But there is still a wedge between us," I told her. My mother has never been the loving mother type. She never saw the good in me, only noticed the things I did wrong.

"It has nothing to do with patience," my father snapped at her. "Although the Gods chose you to be his wife, he has not attached himself to you. But I wouldn't worry about that; I would worry more about the enemy that is sitting on the horizon," he said. The tone in my father's voice was concerning.

"What enemy?" I questioned him

"As we walked into the portal, I could sense a great leader. The queen of all queens. Gethambe's true mate. And he sensed her as well."

"What?" I whispered, tears beginning to fall from my eyes as I dropped my father's dish onto the floor.

"Nothing is written in stone," my mother said, walking over to clean the mess I had just made.

"A queen of all queens? What does that even mean?" I asked, taking a seat at the table.

"The entity that I sensed was filled with old magic. A force to be reckoned with. She would be a valuable asset to our kind. But she would be the savior to the mountain lions. If they were to get their hands on her first, there would be a great battle for land and power," he said, rubbing his hands across the deep waves in his hair.

"What should I do?" I asked my father.

"What do you mean?" my mother snapped. "You are the queen. Gethambe has accepted you. You gave your sacrifice to Lilith for your title and position. You have nothing to worry about."

My father reached over and grabbed my hand and looked at me with pity, "She's coming. Gethambe is going to hunt her down and try to persuade her to be with him.

But you do have an advantage over her. I didn't sense any shape-shifting ability – so, she is not blessed by the elders. And if you have Gethambe's children, he would probably commit himself to you. Family is everything in this pack. But if he submits to you, the pack needs to prepare themselves for a great war. Because if she mates with the lions and become the queen of their pride, she will insist on bringing them out of the darkness and back into the graces of the Gods."

"Nonsense," my mother stated. "No shape-shifting abilities," she laughed. "The Gods would never bless that union."

"Woman, if you don't shut up, I will strangle the life from your body and throw it into the Piranha Nile!" My father yelled, his voice strong and harsh.

She knew better than to say anything else. My father was a man of his word. If he said he would snap your neck, he would snap your neck. That is why he was the leader of the Canine Crew.

My father, Pax, was tall, with smooth chocolate skin and dark eyes. He always looked pissed off, but he was as gentle as a kitten. But he was an excellent executor when it came to him planning an attack, guarding the compound, and retrieving information. He was quick on his toes with answers and quicker on his toes with the solution. No one crossed him, not even our elder king.

"So, what should I do?" I questioned.

"Talk to Samael when you meet with him today. He has the gift of sight and can lead you in the right direction," my father recommended. "But be careful. He is the Archangel of Death, and his actions could be misleading. You don't want to get in the bed with the Devil himself," he warned.

I wish my mother could be more like my father. Even while we were growing up, she cared more about her position as a socialite than she cared about being a mother to her children. Our father not only worked hard in the military, but he was the one who came home and tended to his family.

She was always in town, shopping like the humans, spending the pack's hard-earned money on herself. She was a selfish woman who lusted for power, position, and money. And to be honest, when we were growing up, I didn't even think that she cared about my father. She only produced us to hold on tight to him.

I stood up from the table and leaned in to give my father a gentle kiss on his forehead. He looked at me and smiled. As I began to walk away, he said, jokingly, "If all else fails, there's nothing wrong with becoming Gethambe's concubine."

I couldn't help but laugh at his odd sense of humor. However, I could tell by the look on my mother's face that she didn't like the joke at all. She was such a waste of energy.

As I made my way into the spare bedroom, a feeling of desire hit me like a ton of bricks. And something inside of me said to turn on my mental switch to my beast. So, I stood still, flipped my switch, and listened. The pack was silent; not one person was talking. Without knowing that I possessed the power of astral projection, my body was frozen in time while my spirit shimmered out of it. I could see my body as I levitated into the sky and floated away from Edom. I traveled through a spiral of magnificent rays of vibrant colors, moving at the speed of light until my spirit arrived on earth. My spirit found a host in a hawk and took control over it. I flew over our lands, looking down onto it until I found several members of the Canine Crew lurking around a human home. I glided to a tree, perched on the branch, and watched tentatively as the pack huddled in secrecy.

She must be the one. She had to be the one my father had warned me of. I watched as Rouge left the pack to investigate, stopping every so many steps to look in the windows. When he gathered the information he needed, I saw as he made his way back to the pack that lay behind a small hill.

A moment or two later, I saw what I didn't want to see, my husband in beast form, following Rouge back to the house. As they stood in front of her home, he gazed into the window, looking at her in a way that he had never looked at me before. Desire ran deep in him for her.

When they left, I sat there for a moment to see none other than the lions coming in from a different direction, with Bullet leading the pack. He too must have caught the scent of this magical being and went to investigate.

They were only there for a few minutes before leaving. When the coast was clear, I released the hawk and allowed my spirit to find me. When it arrived back to my body, I fell to the floor, exhausted by the journey.

I can't remember when my mother ever became concerned with my health, but as my vision came back into view, she was sitting on the floor beside me, holding me close to her.

"Where did you go?" she cried. "Where did you go?"

My father stood over me and said, "You have the gift of astral projection and the power to heal." He then fell to his knee and thanked the Gods. "Not many of us can travel across the realms of life and death. And only a handful can do it in spirit," he explained.

"He found her," I said, exhausted from the trip. "And so did the mountain lions."

"Don't get discouraged. When you travel across realms, time is either sped up or slowed down. So, you may be seeing the future, it could be the present, and there is a possibility that it was the past. Regardless, you have a special gift that will win you favor with the Gods."

"Did you not just see what I saw?" my mother questioned, crying enough tears to fill a tub. "Her body was cold as ice as if she was dead, her skin was pale, and her eyes were white like snow!"

"Because she was an empty shell. Go find something to do and get away from me, Cherish!" my father snapped. "You're making me regret the day I married you!"

My mother left me propped up against the wall as she scurried away. My father sat on the floor beside me and pulled me into his arms. He rubbed my head to console me.

"So many things are changing. My body is evolving quickly, giving me more gifts. Is this a good thing?" I asked him.

"It is a blessing," he stated. "The more you can offer, the more valuable you are to that world," he explained.

"More valuable than her?" I needed to know.

"No," he said, shattering my heart. "But valuable enough to keep you from going through the reincarnation cycle if he chooses her over you. The Almighty would place you with another king in a different world. One that could benefit from your gifts."

"But I want the husband that was promised to me," I whimpered.

"My girls don't cry. Straighten that shit up right now, little lady. If you want him, fight for him. Just don't misuse those gifts to keep him," he said to me. "Now get ready for your meeting with Samael."

"We just had breakfast," I said, confused.

"My darling child, you have been gone for hours. When your spirit travels in between worlds and realms, you leave your body for hours or days at a time. It's only minutes when your spirit is traveling in the world your body is located," he explained.

"Daddy, how do you know all of this?" I questioned, wiping my face.

"I have been around for more years than I can count. Jabari wasn't the first king I served. Now go get dressed before you are late," he said, getting up from the floor and helping me up as well.

I hugged my father and went into my room, and selected a traditional outfit for the evening. When in Edom, you're not afforded the luxury of modern clothing. They were nice outfits but lacked the appeal of a designer. Everything worn here was hand-stitched with minimum design. Usually, the clothing here is designed with one of the five elements of life imprinted on it.

After dressing, I hurried to my dinner with Samael. I knew that he was a prompt man and frowned on lateness.

I arrived at the door and was greeted by a servant girl with the prettiest smile I had ever laid my eyes on. Here in Edom, even the servant girls are treated well.

"Come in," she said; her voice was soft and inviting. "He is already in the dining room waiting for you." She then pointed in the direction I was to go.

When I walked in, I found Samael sitting at the head of the table with his two wives on each side of him. Until I walked in, they were in a joyous mood. The laughter stopped as I made my way to the table.

Like tradition, I bowed my head and waited for him to invite me to have a seat.

"Please sit down, Sweet Lana," he grinned.

I took my seat at the other end of the table, facing him and his entourage of wives. Everyone was staring at me curiously, waiting patiently for me to tell them what a train wreck my life had become.

"Nice to see you again, Lilith, Eisheth Zenunim, Na'amah, and Agrat bat Mahlat," I greeted the wives.

"His dick is a big one," Eisheth Zenunim said. All the wives began to laugh in unison, knowing that I had not yet been able to handle my husband's sexual needs.

"Eisheth," Samael said, "Don't be so cruel," he grinned wickedly. "You have to forgive my wives; I didn't teach them any manners," he laughed.

"It is true," I responded, trying to make this dinner as

quick as possible. "Gethambe is so large that he rips me every time we become intimate."

"You have to tame the beast," Na'amah said. "Stupid girl. You don't have a clue about seducing the man and wielding the beast."

"No, ma'am. Because the beast keeps making his appearance in our bed when Gethambe becomes too excited," I explained. "I feel that if I could learn to please my husband, he would love me more and accept our union," I said.

"No. He won't," Samael answered. "You disgust him. Although you leak the hormones that should pull him to you, it is the very thing that is pushing him away. Gethambe has a taste for human pussy." As he placed his hands onto the table, his eyes turned cherry red, and his skin illuminated in a vibrant gold color. "She will come like a thief in the night to steal his heart, and Gethambe will give it to her willingly. Together, they will have many children and rule as equals. She will be the one to set the rebellion in motion, uniting the wolves and lions as one. She will show strength and have a love of the people," he said, as his body slowly changed from a glowing light of sunshine back to normal.

Samael looked at me curiously. I looked back at him with fear dancing in my eyes. "Do your visions always come true?" I asked him.

"Although I can see the future, there is always room for change. I can only see what's going to happen right now. But tomorrow, something as insignificant as the shirt that you choose to wear can change its outcome."

"So, there's a possibility that I will win my husband's heart, and together we will rule as equals?"

"Silly queen," Agrat bat Mahlat chimed in. "You don't have the backbone to command a beast like Gethambe. You're so worried about satisfying his needs that you have become weak," she said; her voice was cold and harsh. Then all the wives laughed at me again. "Accept the fact that you were dealt a losing hand." Then she excused herself from the table with the other wives following in her footsteps.

"Go home, new queen. Fix what is broken, and he just may choose you," Samael said. "But here's a little tip for you." He stood up and walked down to the end of the table where I sat. "Have several candles made especially for your den. You want them to use lavender, chamomile, and peppermint in equal parts. And before you become intimate with your husband, light them. Let the aroma engulf your den. Then mate with him. Those elements calm the beast within him and hide the scent that expels from your body. He is still going to sniff you, but the candles will fool his senses."

Samael started for the door but stopped abruptly. He turned to me and said, "Remember this old wise saying by Jean Nidetch – Its choice, not chance, that determines your destiny."

He smiled and then disappeared. As I sat there alone, the young servant girl arrived with a salad that was prepared and sent to me by Lilith herself. It looked so good that my mouth watered.

"Lilith said the salad with pumpkin seeds, salmon, and

olive oil will help you to become pregnant. And she said that it would be considered as rude not to accept her gift."

That was something Lilith didn't have to worry about. I wanted to have my husband's child, and if this is what helped, she should have sent a second helping.

10

ASHLEY

I have been sitting around this house drinking, trying to forget that awkward encounter with my ex-husband. Yeah, he made me feel good for a few minutes, then he hit me with the news that he was going home to his bitch. It made me sick to my stomach knowing that another woman was able to step into my life and take what belonged to me. Before my scandalous divorce, I thought William was my soulmate. I knew I had him wrapped around my finger and that no other bitch had a chance. Wasn't I wrong?

There wasn't much to do around here besides donating your money to the casino. So, to keep myself from going stir crazy, I'm going to put down this bottle of vodka, pull myself together, and go out for the night and hopefully meet a nice gentleman to take my mind off William. I thought about inviting Kwan, but I wasn't that desperate. At least not right now.

It didn't take me any time to perfect my look. I wore a fuzzy white sweater that hung off one shoulder and a pair of black leggings. Because I wanted to be comfortable, I slid into a pair of knee-high boots with a small heel on them. I pulled my hair up into a high ponytail and spiraled some baby hair around my edges. I added some black liner and glitter gloss to bring out my beautiful eyes and plump lips. I grabbed my handbag and keys and made my way to the door.

As I opened the door to step out, I was shocked by the gorgeous god that was standing there about to knock on it. He was tall, with a muscular physique and a smile that made me cream.

"My car stopped on me down the street. Do you have a phone I could use?" he said.

"Sure," I answered, mesmerized by his thick accent and long, straight, black hair.

We stood there looking at each other, neither of us breaking eye contact. "This is awkward," he smiled, still standing at my door.

"I'm sorry," I giggled. "Come in." Normally, I didn't invite people into my home that I didn't know, especially a man. But something about him seemed trustworthy.

"By the way, my name is Bullet," he introduced himself.

"Ashley," I responded, extending my hand for a handshake.

He looked down at my hand and extended his. He pulled my hand up to his mouth and kissed the back of it gently.

"It's a pleasure to meet you, Ashley," he said.

As my eyes took in his masculine physique, I inadvertently stopped at his waist when I noticed the prominent bulge in his pants. I couldn't help but gasp when I saw it.

"Where can I find the phone?" I heard him ask.

"What?" I replied, with my eyes still glued to his package.

"The phone," I heard him laugh.

"Oh, yeah," I giggled, embarrassed because I knew he had to see my eyes locked on his dick.

I took him into my living room and pointed to the phone. As he walked past me, I was immediately drawn to the smell of his Giorgio Armani Rose cologne. I used to buy that for William, so I knew that fragrance well.

After we were married, he sprayed it on the sheets for me when he wasn't home. He used to tell me that it was so that I would never feel alone.

I took a seat on the couch and waited patiently while he telephoned a friend. I didn't think I would find a native man attractive, but Lord, everyone I have come into contact with has been breathtaking. It was something about that long silky hair and that devastating sand-colored skin that was driving me crazy.

He hung up the phone and looked at me disappointedly. "I know you don't know me, but could I bother you for a small favor?" he asked.

Yes, Mr. Native Guy, I would happily bend over and let you ram all that dick into me, I thought to myself. "Sure," I answered, thinking about various positions I would allow him to put me into.

"My friend can't come and get me right now, and it's hot as hell outside...would it be possible to sit here and wait for him?" he asked.

Before I could catch the words that were falling from my mouth, I answered, "Sure."

He took a seat across from me and said, "I truly appreciate this. I promise you this isn't a gimmick or anything like that, and I'm not a psycho-killer either," he laughed.

"I believe you," I replied. "Are you hungry? Or thirsty?" I inquired.

"What do you have?" he smiled. I haven't had the time to grab anything to eat, and I would love a cold glass of water."

"Well, I don't cook much, but I'm sure I can make a sandwich for you while you wait, and luckily for you, I paid my water bill this month," I returned a smile to him.

I got up, not forgetting to take my purse, and made my way to my bedroom before going to the kitchen. I didn't want to leave my purse lying around with all my money and credit cards in it. He seemed nice, but you really couldn't trust people nowadays.

I made my way to the kitchen and fixed my guest a ham and cheese sandwich, and fetched him a glass of ice water. I walked back into the living room to find him sitting in the same place I left him. So, if he was looking for something to steal, he was doing a piss poor job of it.

I happily handed him the plate of food and a glass of water. As I leaned forward, the necklace I was wearing fell from my shirt and dangled in front of him. He looked at it and admired its beauty.

"That's an unusual piece of jewelry," he said, accepting the food and water.

I walked back over to the couch, sat down, and began to

fumble with it. "It's been in our family for years," I said. "My mother loved wolves, her grandmother loved wolves, and her grandmother before her. So, when my mother passed away, I had her cremated per her wishes and had them insert some of her ashes into the two interlocking wolves," I explained.

"I've seen that symbol before," he said. "It's an old myth around here about the wolves," he stated, biting into his sandwich.

My eyes widened with curiosity, and Bullet had my undivided attention. "What type of myth?" I asked.

"Well, it was said that back in ancient times, the wolves were blessed by the Gods to maintain balance in these lands, and the mountain lions were the protectors. The first king of the wolves was a hybrid and the same for the first mountain lion. The first hybrid wolf was a third of human-ity, a third of demi-god, and a third of wolf. The mountain lion needed to be fiercer, so he was only cut into two parts, half-man and half-lion. Together, they fought side by side, caring for and protecting the land until the mountain lion king turned his back on his people. He supposedly sold his soul to the devil to lead the army of the condemned dead against the archangels. The mountain lion people were punished for his greed for power, and the wolves were blessed for remaining loyal to their god."

"So, what does that have to do with the two interlocking wolves on my necklace?" I questioned, leaning forward as I ran the locket from side to side on the chain.

"That is the family crest of the first shape-shifter created. How your grandparents were able to get their hands on something so valuable is beyond me," he answered, taking the last gulp of water from his glass.

I thought about what he was saying and how cool it would be to have a shape-shifter family tree. I would love to be considered royalty. But I personally thought all this shit was hogwash. There were no such things as ghosts, demons, demi-gods, or werewolves. I felt that someone had an over-active imagination and made millions of dollars from the storyline.

"Well, that was an interesting story, and I thank you for the entertainment," I said, laughing.

"People around here believe in those legends and would be offended if you were to tell them that it wasn't true," his face became pale as if he saw a ghost.

"What is it?" I asked. His look had startled me.

"I think I hear a car coming down your driveway."

Shit. I felt my heart jump out of my chest, thinking I was about to be taken by the Hob Goblin or something.

He stood and made his way to the door. I followed him, inhaling his cologne that brought back some sweet memories. He opened the door and began to walk out when I said, "I don't know anyone here. Maybe you could show me around. I was just on my way to the casino if you would like to join me."

He looked back at me, and I could see delight was written all over his face. Within the brief time that we had spent together, he had become smitten with my company. I had that effect on men. I was drop-dead gorgeous, with an attractive body and an incredible personality. And judging by the look on his face, I wasn't even worried about him saying no.

"I'm not a gambling man, but I know where we could find a decent meal that offers a quiet and intimate atmosphere," he answered.

"Let me grab my purse," I replied, running into the house to grab my bag. I made sure that I had my pepper spray ready just in case he thought he was going to steal my sweetness before it was offered to him.

He told his ride to pick him up around seven which I thought was odd. If we were going out together, why is it that he didn't want me to take him home? I hope this fool isn't married. I don't have the time or patience to deal with this type of shit with all I have been through.

We hopped into my car, and as we drove down my driveway, I noticed a pack of wolves huddled together off in the distance. Simultaneously, all five of them watched my car as I slowly rode down my driveway. To see that all ten eyes were looking at me sent a slight hint of fear racing through me. I knew that they were close, but I didn't realize exactly how close they were.

"Don't be afraid; they won't attack you," Bullet said. "They very seldom come around people. They're probably out scavenging for food, and the car scared them."

"It's just that I didn't know they were that close to me."

"You have a newly built home, and it's probably near their den."

"So, do I need to do anything special to keep them away?" I asked.

"Yeah. Don't open your door when the wolf comes knocking," he laughed.

"As big as those damn things are, you don't have to worry about that."

Bullet directed me to a historic brick building in downtown Winslow. They must have offered decent food because the place was packed. So much so that I found it hard to find a parking spot. Since there was virtually nothing available, Bullet directed me to park in the space for the employee of the month. I felt guilty for doing it, but I didn't want to have to walk a country mile to get to the damn place.

As soon as I placed the car into park, Bullet hopped out and raced around to my side to open the door for me. Like Kwan, he was a gentleman. He extended his hand, helped me out, and then shut the door behind us. We walked side by side to the door, where he opened it for me and stood to the side as I walked in first.

The restaurant was dimly lit with strobe lighting, soft jazz played in the background, and a citrus smell engulfed the small building.

"Hey Bullet, we miss you around here," the greeter announced, giving Bullet a bro hug.

"Meet Ashley," he introduced. "She has that new home that was built on Old Route Sixty-Six."

Without asking, he pulled me into him and hugged me. If I wasn't mistaken, I could swear he sniffed me several times before letting me go. Then he looked at me as if I were on the menu, making me feel like I was a tad bit underdressed.

"Nice to meet you, Ashley, and welcome to The Lion's Den," he smiled.

"Nice to meet you as well."

He looked at me again and then back over at Bullet. He motioned for us to follow him to a table that sat in the middle of the restaurant, surrounded by couples that were in love. The greeter pulled out my chair and then handed me the menu. Once Bullet sat down, he gave him one as well.

"Should I start you off with a nice red wine?" he asked.

I could feel my heart jump for joy. Finally, a place that offers red wine. "What do you have?"

"We just got a shipment in today of Hazlitt, Sweet Red Cat, Madame."

With that, I was ready to get up and leave. I was so tired of drinking cheap red wine. It was rough on my stomach and sometimes gave me gas. My body wasn't built for this shit. But I wanted a drink, and I lived alone. So, I can pass gas all night long without bothering a soul.

"I'll have a glass, please."

"And what about you, Bullet?"

"I'll just take a draft beer."

He smiled again at us before walking away. "Okay, your friend is a little creepy."

"He gets excited when he meets new people. Winslow is a small town."

"So, I've noticed," I tried to say quietly under my breath.

"Too small for the city girl, huh?" he laughed.

"Too small and too slow for my liking. But I must admit,

it's slowly growing on me," I answered, placing the napkin into my lap.

"Well, I'm sorry to disappoint you, but it doesn't get any better than this," he laughed. "Where are you from anyway?"

"Jacksonville, Florida. Although my family originated from right here in Winslow."

"What is the family's last name?"

"Notah," I answered. But I wished I hadn't. It seemed as if the whole restaurant stopped talking and began listening to our conversation.

"Okay," he said. "The Notah family name goes way back."

"Like as in my people were slaves?" I joked. I'm a black woman, and I am very knowledgeable about the history of my people.

"No. Like as in shape-shifters," he answered as we were being served our drinks.

"Are you ready to order?" the greeter asked.

"Just a house salad for me."

"The Philly Cheesesteak sandwich for me with fries."

He nodded his head and made his way to the kitchen. But another unsettling feeling came over me when five massive, absolutely handsome men walked into the restaurant. Their presence demanded attention, and they received it. All eyes were on them, and my mind was glued to the hunk that was leading the bunch.

They made their way over to our table, and Mr. Mysterious looked at me hungrily. His eyes were chewing away at my soul, making me melt like butter. I have never seen so many fine-ass men under one roof. I felt like God had blessed me.

"Hello, beautiful. My name is Gethambe."

"Ashley," I said, blushing from the attention I was receiving. But I wasn't trying to be rude to my date, so I introduced him as well. "And this is –"

"Bullet," he interrupted.

So, both hunks knew each other. How fucking sweet is that.

Bullet stood up and faced Gethambe and asked him to leave his establishment. "You have no right to be here," he said. "This is our land."

Gethambe's chest swelled as his words roared from his it. "Fuck you nigga. And if you have any friends, fuck them too. I go where I want and when I want, bitch ass motherfucker."

I don't know what I had just gotten myself into, but this shit was scaring the hell out of me. I politely removed the napkin from my lap and placed it back on the table. I grabbed my purse and stood up, "Uhm, I'm going to go now. Maybe I will see you around town," I said to Bullet.

He didn't acknowledge me. Bullet's eyes were locked in a fierce battle with Gethambe's. So, my words fell on deaf ears.

"If you feel froggy, leap bitch," Gethambe taunted. When Bullet didn't make a move to defend himself, Gethambe and his crew laughed. "I didn't think so. Bitch ass nigga."

I didn't want to stay there and be caught in the middle of a fight, so I eased my way to the door and out to my car.

Before I could open the door, Gethambe was standing behind me.

His presence soothed me, gave me comfort, and eased my troubled soul. I didn't know anything about this man, but I wanted to.

"Let me take you home," his voice was gentle, not like the thunderous roar I had just heard in the restaurant. I turned to look at him and was captivated by his dark eyes, long black hair, and muscular build. The way his words slid from his lips hypnotized me as if he was singing a seductive love ballad. And although he wore no cologne, his scent made my nub throb with want. What was it about him?

"I'm okay," I said; my voice was barely a whisper.

"Then let us follow you home to make sure you make it to your door unharmed," he insisted.

"Okay," I agreed. I could feel my heart pounding against my chest with desire. I was so mesmerized by his presence that I couldn't think straight. He had bewitched me without me knowing it.

He took the keys from my hand, placed his hand on the small of my back, and led me to the passenger side of my own car. Gethambe opened my door, and I got in without question. He got into the driver's side and started my car. Within seconds, we were racing down the highway to my house.

I didn't have to give him any directions; he knew where I lived and how to get there. I didn't ask how; I was just satisfied with being with him. Gethambe, I repeated in my head.

We pulled up to my home, and he got out of the car and

came around to my side. He opened it for me and helped me out. He walked me to my door and opened it for me.

"Be careful who you allow into your life," he warned, planting a soft, luxurious, sweet kiss onto my lips. Just the touch of his hand when he pulled my chin up to him sent waves of ecstasy pulsating throughout my veins. And when his tongue interlocked with mine, I came. It was only a kiss, and I fucking came a river. *What the fuck?*

He reached down between my legs and rubbed my wetness. I didn't try to push his hand back; instead, I let him continue to stroke it. Then he pulled his hand away from my sweet spot and sniffed it. It must have smelled good enough to eat because he dropped to his knees and rubbed his face against it, taking in deep breaths and licking my lady through my leggings.

When he heard the howling of the wolves, he stopped. "Go inside and lock your door. I will be back shortly to see you again," his voice was low and desperate.

I didn't want him to stop. I wanted him to eat me like dinner and fuck me hard and fast. But he had to go. So, I backed into my house, leaving him on his knees at my front door, and I closed and locked it as he directed.

GETHAMBE

I stood at the portal of life and waited for Lana to arrive. My heart was heavy with regret because I realized I didn't love her. I know that I don't know the human girl well, but she smells and feels right. Just the few minutes that I spent inhaling her scent made my dick swell in want. I have a craving for her sweetness, but I'm unsure if she can satisfy it. We are two different species. Regardless of our diverse backgrounds, I'm still willing to try, though.

As the portal opened and my wife appeared, I could feel that something was different with her. When she walked out of the portal and into the den, her head was held high, and her demeanor was pure confidence. Lana walked up to me and gave me a gentle kiss on my cheek, and asked me to meet her in our chambers within the hour.

"I'll be waiting, My Love," she said, with a smile of sheer wickedness.

I sort of knew what it was; she said that she would handle all this dick and rock my world when she returned. Well, shit hasn't changed here but the day of the week.

Although her scent makes me sick to my stomach, I have to admit that she has some sweet, tight pussy that makes a man feel like a man. It doesn't hurt either that her body is banging.

When she walked away, I could see that my loyal soldiers were flipping their switch off from their beast. You can tell when it happens because you must close your eyes and bow your head. You need to concentrate on disengaging for the switch to flip off. Then your mind is your own, and it is free from chatter.

"Queen Lana seems a little different," Rouge said.

"Yeah, I noticed that. I was thinking that she was a little more confident."

"We heard what you were thinking," Joker stated, laughing uncontrollably.

"Nigga, shut the fuck up," I told him, smiling because he was right. My mind was deep in the gutter, and the whole pack heard my thoughts.

"I don't know, King Gethambe, I think she knows about the humanoid," Stewart confessed.

"I think she does too," Juice agreed. "She has the power of the beast as well. And when your nose and tongue were sniffing and tasting her, even my dick got hard with want."

"I'm going to tell her. She wants to meet in about an hour, so I will tell her then. I don't want to hurt her, but she's not right for me. I want the human."

"I'm not trying to rain on your parade, but isn't that forbidden?" Rouge asked. He was like Lana's father, straightforward all the time. But he was his son, after all. I kind of felt like shit that I was about to break his sister's heart. But he understood the nature of the beast. You can't control what the heart wants, and the Gods can't always predict a perfect match.

"The Gods don't promote it, they prefer that we stay with our own, but they don't forbid it," I explained. "My problem is they have accepted Lana, and we were married. They are not a fan of separation. I can have other women sexually because I'm the Alpha, but technically, we are to be mated for life," I told them.

"So, are you bold enough to go against the Gods for a piece of pussy?" Juice asked.

"For that piece of pussy – hell yeah!"

I gave my boys a fist bump and made my way to my chamber to face the music. Lana didn't deserve what I was about to do to her. But she deserved to be with a king that would love and cherish their union. When I told my parents that Lana didn't smell right, I should have stood my ground and not proceeded with the marriage. I didn't have to accept her because the Gods felt that she was the one. But I did in honor of our traditions.

I opened the door, and a very tantalizingly and beautiful Lana greeted my eyes. The room was surrounded by candles that exuded a calming aroma. I knew one scent was lavender, but I couldn't make out the other aromas that were mingled with it. As I stepped through the doorway, my eyes rested on Lana's smooth, delectable curves, and I became aroused just by the sight of her body. She stood at the foot of our bed with nothing on except a sheer robe that she had left open, revealing her succulent breasts.

I could see her dark, erect nipples, her smooth copper

skin, and her shaven, inviting sacred garden. Although my intentions tonight had been to tell her about the human girl, I could no longer bring myself to do it. The only thing I could think about was the wetness between her legs.

I walked over to her and grabbed her breasts in my hands, and squeezed them gently. She stood there silently and watched me as I passionately caressed them. Then she placed her hand on my shoulder and pushed me down onto my knees as she disrobed.

My eyes turned cherry red with desire, and my skin burned with lust. Although I had done this so many times before, I still pushed my nose into her pussy and flickered it across her nub. Her juices began to spill into my mouth freely, and I could tell that she was ready to accept me. Somehow, the smell that usually nauseated me so badly was missing. She had masked it with the scent of the candles that she had burning in our chambers.

I drank happily from her, howling as I became more aroused. She tossed one of her legs over my shoulder and gripped the back of my head, pulling me in close to her. Her nectar was sweet and plentiful; she leaked uncontrollably. I never suckled from a woman's sweet spot, but I was mesmerized by this seductive show that lured me to her.

I pulled her second leg onto my other shoulder and stood up as I began to suck on her nub and lick it savagely. I held onto her by her legs, and she held onto me by my head.

"Yes. Yes. Yes. My Love. Eat it up," she moaned as she slowly gyrated her hips.

My dick stiffened with excitement, and I felt my blood coursing eagerly through my veins.

I needed to be inside of her. I needed to feel her tightness strangle my dick as it massaged it gently. So, I turned to face the bed and tossed her onto it. Her body went sailing through the air, and she deftly maneuvered herself, landing on her hands and knees.

I looked at her and laughed to myself, thinking, *this bitch has upgraded her game since her visit to Edom.*

I watched her intently as she crawled around in a circle on our bed like a prowling feline, stopping when she had made a complete rotation. Then, she sat up on her knees and opened her legs. Purring, she pointed to her kitty and then to me.

I tore out of my clothes, freeing my manhood. It was long, thick, and pulsating eagerly with lust for her. I held it in my hand and looked at Lana. Immediately, she smiled. She knew what I wanted. I had tasted her cream, but now it was her turn to taste mine.

She crawled over to me and sat on the edge of the bed. She wrapped her soft, delicate hands around my shaft and pulled the head of my dick into her mouth. Lana sucked on it and licked it like a lollipop, letting her saliva sloppily drip from her mouth and stream between her breasts.

"I'm too old of a cat to be fucked by a pussy," I told her. "Deep throat me bitch!" I howled, wanting to feel the back of her throat graze the head of my cock.

With the tip of my dick in her mouth, she looked up at me and swallowed my shaft – inch by motherfucking inch. Watching her take me down her throat excited every nerve in my body.

"Dammit, Lana," I growled. "What's changed?"

With my dick lodged firmly between her lips, she wasn't able to respond. As she began to work her way back to my tip, I could feel drops of my warm pre-cum seeping out and dripping onto her wet, twisting tongue.

She scooted back onto the bed and opened her legs wide for me. This would be the moment of truth. Usually, when I'm deep inside of her, she is unable to handle it. Lana spends most of the time running from me instead of enjoying the moment.

I crawled into the bed and positioned my length between her legs. I laid on top of her, showering her with passionate kisses. I wanted to give her that much before I ripped her ass in half.

Without warning, I grabbed my dick and pierced her core in one swift thrust. She tried to pull away, but I pulled her back down and held her in place.

"Gethambe!" she yelled. "Oh, Baby!"

I loved hearing her scream – it made my dick harder. I continued to push into her until I was completely submerged in her sweetness. I laid still for a few minutes, letting her accommodate my throbbing cock.

She was panting and moaning, and a lone tear ran down from her eye. I dipped my head down and gently licked it away, just as I had done on our wedding night. I couldn't deny the beauty of this woman, and I couldn't deny how good she felt wrapped securely around me. But I had to remember that we were on two totally different wavelengths as far as our relationship. Lana wanted that unconditional love, and I wanted a woman that I was attracted to mentally, physically, and emotionally.

I started to slowly thrust into her with a smooth, precise stride. She wrapped her arms around my neck, and I kissed her lips gently. I felt her try to swirl her hips against my manhood, but I was too much for her.

"You're so deep," she moaned. "Too deep."

I only smiled and increased the speed of my stroke.

"Mmmmh," she moaned again. "I love you,"

I responded by beginning to pound viciously in her. I did not do this to hurt her, but because I wanted to reach my climax as quickly as possible. When she said that she loved me, my mind wandered to the human girl. My eyes welled – I wanted her so badly, but here I was, settling for a quick nut with Lana.

I grabbed her hips and thumped into her pussy hard, pounding into her sweet spot with no mercy or care for her pained cries. When she tried to pull away from me again, I bit down on her neck, piercing her with my sharp canines. I snaked my arm around her body, and my claws dug deep into her skin.

I had immobilized her and used her body for my own selfish pleasure. As I tiptoed onto the Rock of Gibraltar and began to dive into the rushing waterfall of euphoria, I howled out in ecstasy. My heart pounded savagely against my chest, and my breathing was heavy. Lust and guilt washed through me, wave after wave. Despite the confusion I felt, my heated cum was begging to be released from its prison.

I heard Lana whine softly, and that was enough to push me over the edge. I exploded into her like an atomic bomb – my nectar shot from my cock, spurting strings of my warm, sticky load deep inside of her. My body bucked wildly, my balls tightened, and my toes curled as I emptied myself into her.

I released her neck and buried my head in her hair, tears pouring from my eyes. The guilt had come rushing back. As my beast retracted, I held her close to me for comfort.

"Sssshhh, Baby," she whispered. "I'm fine. I have a cream for the cuts, and the bleeding will stop soon." Her neck was bloody from where I dug my teeth into it.

"Lana. I don't love you," I murmured. "I feel like I need to be with the human girl whose scent pulls me into her being."

"What!" she yelled. "Get off me! Get off me, Geth-ambe!" she continued, hitting me repeatedly with her tiny fist.

"I can't, Lana. I'm still swollen inside of you," I tried to explain, but she didn't hear my words. She was enraged, still fighting me as she cried. When she lost the strength to fight, she just lay under me and cried more.

I held her close to me, trying to ease her pain. But I was unsuccessful at my attempt. She turned her head to the side and wouldn't even look at me. Although I didn't love her the way she wanted and needed, I didn't want to hurt her like this.

When I was able to pull out of her, I got up and walked over to the basin to clean myself up. I bought back a warm cloth to clean her wounds, but she lay there motionless, staring off into the great unknown.

"Someday, you will make someone a great queen. But you're not the queen for me."

"How could you love a human? Someone who knows nothing about us, our people; who knows nothing about our kind?" she asked. The tone in her voice was empty.

"I don't know," I answered her honestly.

"Then how do you know she is who you want?" Lana wanted to know, with desolation deep within her.

"I visited her while you were away. While there, I tasted her juices, and she imprinted on me. Her scent is right, her cream is delicious, and she melts my heart without even trying," I explained.

"I saw you," she whispered. "I saw you there."

"How? You were in Edom."

"Because I was granted the power of astral projection. And I flew in the body of a hawk and watched as you spied on your whore."

I continued to wipe the blood from my wife. When I finished cleaning her wounds, I changed the bed while she still laid in it. I dressed her in a clean gown and kissed her on her forehead.

"I will be moving into the whore's chambers. I have no desire to become intimate with you anymore. I will call upon Samael and tell him of my decision and face the wrath of the Gods," I said to her.

Lana closed her eyes without acknowledging a word I said. I gathered some things I needed and proceeded to my new chambers.

12

LANA

We put on a fake face for our people, but they talked in secret about our issues. I am so embarrassed, and rage is running rampant throughout my body. I want to kill this human bitch, but I will be shunned from the pack if I do.

He thinks that I don't know about his rendezvous with her. He leaves daily with a party of his loyal soldiers to spend a couple of hours with her. He's not even trying to keep her a secret anymore. Even when they are together, I can hear his thoughts, feel his emotions, and understand his desire, because he doesn't bother to flip his switch to his beast.

Gethambe said he didn't want to hurt me, so why is he allowing me to hear what he says to her and what he feels about this worthless human? If he cared about me at least a little, he would respect the fact that I am still his mated wife and do his dirt without including me in his emotions.

"Excuse me, Queen Lana," the chambermaid said, her voice low and her head down.

"It is a rule that you don't speak to me with your head lowered," I snapped, listening to Gethambe as he cooed all over the human named Ashley.

"I have the results you requested," she said, smiling at me.

I took the stick from her hand and saw the plus sign. My eyes widened with delight as I yelled telepathically, *"I'm pregnant!"*

"What?" Gethambe replied.

"It has been confirmed. I am carrying your pup or pups," I laughed.

Then he disconnected his wolf, leading me to think that he didn't give a fuck about the seed that he planted in my womb. And if he chose her over his own pups, I'm sure the Gods would side with me and kick him from our pack. But that's not what I wanted. I want him to come home and be with me. I want him to treat me as he treats her, with love and respect. I want my husband to be a husband and stop all this foolishness with this girl who could never give him what I could offer him. She's human.

"My Lady," I heard another voice say. "Samael is waiting for you in the formal dining room." She bowed and walked out.

I know it might seem raunchy of me to involve him in this messy situation with Gethambe and me, but I have no other options. My husband has moved out of our bed and spends a lot of time outside the walls of our society. He isn't a king nor a husband.

I made my way to the dining room and curtsied to Samael.

"Why did you call for me, Lana? I have given you all the pointers I have to help you satisfy your husband," he said, motioning for the servant to bring him some wine.

I walked over to the table and took a seat close to him. Before the servant girl could pour wine into my glass, I covered it with my hand and shooed her away.

"Awe...I see now," Samael grinned. "You are with pups?"

"I am with pups," I repeated, smiling devilishly.

"And Gethambe is with the human?" he said.

"And my husband spends many days with this human."

"Are you jealous?" he questioned. "That could be a bad trait for a queen to become jealous of her husband's extracurricular activities."

"But she is not of this pack. She is human, Samael," I reminded him.

"There is no law that states that he can't have a human girl. Sex is sex," he said nonchalantly. "She may have his heart, but you're wearing the crown."

"Samael, my dear. He has moved out of our shared chambers and into the whore's chamber."

"And there is no law saying that he has to share a bed with you."

"I called you here to help me, not defend his actions. I want my husband to be a husband!" I yelled.

"Disrespectful, are we?" he questioned. "Your childish temper tantrum won't get you anywhere with me. I have four wives to deal with daily and what you're doing right now isn't shit compared to them."

I had to calm myself and try to bring this conversation

back around to the point that Samael would be on my side and willing to give me information about how to get my husband under control. So, I stood up and walked behind him, running my finger across his shoulder, across the back of his neck, before leaning into him and whispering, "What could I do to get my husband back into my chamber and into my bed?" Then I kissed him on his cheek.

He pulled me around him and onto his lap. He looked at me and responded, "Don't tempt me, young queen. I couldn't care less about the pups you carry in your stomach. I would shove my twelve-inch dick up your ass and make you spit cum from your mouth."

I pulled away from him and took my seat back at the table. I was feeling hopeless, dipped in defeat, and it wasn't fair. I had trained my whole life for this moment to be queen and to be his wife. Now I have to face the fact that I may lose my husband to a less suitable woman.

"Is there nothing you can tell me?" I cried.

Samael grabbed the table, his eyes turned white, and his skin illuminated a vibrant color of gold. He was quiet for a few seconds and then said, "Gethambe has made his decision. He will rule as a just king with the half-breed at his side. He will get the approval of the Almighty, and they will be wed. Together, they will unite the mountain lions and the wolves. Both will live in tranquility. BUT, I see trouble darkening his happiness that could bring about a great war. You, my queen, are the trouble that I see. A decision you will make can cause the destruction of your people and the uprising of the mountain lions. Choose your next steps wisely," he warned. Then his skin and eyes returned to normal.

"So, I will destroy this pack because my husband is gallivanting around town with a human?" I asked, pissed about what I had learned.

"Remember the old wise saying I told you while you were in Edom. Jean Nidetch said – It's choice, not chance, which determines your destiny. You need to be careful of your choices and stop allowing jealousy and envy to interfere with your destiny. There are plenty of packs that allow multiple wives; just one chooses to be the Alpha Female. Invite the enemy into your home and make her a friend. Then, you're conquering two problems at once. You're giving your husband what he wants, and he will then give you what you need."

I had to sit back and think that over. Give him what he wants so I can have what I need. I don't mind sharing him; it's the nature of the beast to have multiple partners.

"But what if I invite her into our den, and he still is with her more than he is with me?" I asked. "I can share him, but could she?"

"Jesus, young queen. Can't you figure anything out on your own?"

"Yes. But I'm vibing with your brain at this moment."

"It doesn't matter who spends the majority of the time with him. You will still reign as his queen. She would be nothing more than his second wife. And we all know that the first wife has the power. Like with me, Lilith is my favorite wife, and I spend much of my time in the comforts of her arms. I would give her the heavens if I possessed the power.

But Eisheth Zenunim is my first wife. She is the one who dictates what she will and will not accept from the other wives. They all know their role and their place. And if she were to become a part of your pack, she would have to understand the laws of nature. It's just that simple," he explained.

"So, allow a human to live here, among the wolves, and treat her like family?"

"Allow the half-breed to live here amongst her people where you can keep an eye on her but also keep the mountain lions from obtaining her gifts. That's all I'm saying, dear."

"You keep saying that half-breed shit. What is she?" I was curious. I thought that she was human.

"What makes her so desirable and her scent so strong is, she is a third wolf, a third demi-god, and a third human. I need to do more research on her to find out about her roots. But she is more than capable of mating with Gethambe and probably better suited."

"Is there anything else you want to tell me?" I asked. He was depressing me more and more. "And why can't Gethambe smell the wolf in her?"

"Because it lies dormant in her genes. It has not been awakened, and she does not know."

"As he finished his sentence, Gethambe rushed in with his loyal pack of idiots, my brother included. Rouge was more devoted to his king than he was to his sister.

Gethambe walked into the room with suspicion in his eyes. He walked over to me and looked down at me with hatred. I could hear him now; he was loud and clear.

"So, you went behind my back and called the elders yourself?"

"No, My Love, he just dropped in to check on us," I lied, hoping that Samael would play along. Although he didn't have the gift of telepathy, he could sense the uneasiness in the air.

"Gethambe, I just dropped in to congratulate you on this joyous occasion."

"My wife summoned you, Samael?" Gethambe questioned.

"As a matter of fact, she did. She wanted to discuss that nasty little problem she has been having with you in bed. I had Lilith mix her up a cream that would heal the cuts and wounds quickly. It will also help her to stretch to your needs more efficiently," he said, looking down at Gethambe's bulge. "My wives would just love to have a piece of you. Unfortunately for them, I wasn't as blessed," he sneered.

"He's lying, Lana. What did you tell him?" Gethambe questioned.

"I told him of your whore!" I yelled. My voice was so loud that the pack started to howl.

"Well, it was nice visiting, but I must go home now. Besides, I can't take all the mental arguing; you both are giving me a headache," and he shimmered away.

"Flip your switch, Lana!" Gethambe demanded, and I complied.

"We're pregnant," I said, trying to switch gears on where the conversation was heading.

"Leave us," he told the others. They bowed and left us in the dining room alone.

"Let's set some ground rules here. I'm the Alpha Male, the king, and you are nothing more than a piece of pussy for me to fuck because I cannot become intimate with the human girl. So, know your role and stay in your fucking place. Secondly, when I am in town spending time with the woman *I Love*, flip your fucking beast off because what I say and do with her will only hurt you more. Lastly, if you ever summon one of the elders without my permission again, I will break your fucking neck and suffer the consequences. Is this understood?" his voice was booming and stern.

"Yes, My Love. I will comply," I humbled myself to him.

"Now spill your guts, woman. What did you say to him?" Gethambe took a seat at the table while I remained standing.

"He told me to invite your half-breed into our home and give you the pleasure of having us both." I snitched on myself.

"Half-breed? Ashley is human."

"Your spidey senses must be malfunctioning, My Love. According to Samael, she is a third wolf, a third demi-god, and a third human," I informed him.

"Now I can take her as my wife, and we could lead the pack together," he said, forgetting that I was already his wife.

"And what about me?" I questioned. "I am your first wife, and I am the one carrying your pups. Am I to be tossed out like trash?"

He looked at me and motioned for me to take a seat at the table. "I want you to surrender your crown to her. I care about you, Lana, but I don't love you. I'm completely and totally in love with Ashley. I want to marry her and give her a noble title. I will raise my pups with her; I will ensure that they will be taken care of. But you need to either agree to be recycled or moved to another realm to become a queen for someone who would respect you as such," he said to me with a cold heart. He wanted me to just walk away and leave him and her to raise our children. That won't ever happen, and the Gods will never allow it.

"Gethambe, this is my home too. And I did everything that I was supposed to do. I fought the battles and sacrificed my first unborn daughter for this union. And you want me to just walk away? Leave you with my children and just walk away? How cold could you be?"

"Lana," he said. "Don't you want to be happy? I can't give you that. When we mate, it's pity sex, no love. And we both know if it weren't for the candles you use to hide your scent, immediately afterward, I would throw up. Maybe you are happy. Maybe you find happiness in my misery. But I can't go on like this," he said to me.

"Well. Let me be clear about this, My Love. I'm not leaving my pack. And if you go to the Gods whimpering like a little bitch, they are going to laugh at you and take your precious crown away. The only way you are going to be rid of me is through death," I said, slamming my fist against the table.

Gethambe stood up and shifted into his beast. His coat was pure white, his fangs were long and sharp, and his body was huge and toned. He walked up to me, cocked his hind leg up, and pissed. He shot it into my face, down my body, and on my legs. This was the ultimate disrespect. Males do that to mark a female from being pursued by another male. Gethambe did this just to be nasty. He had just given me my first golden shower, the bastard. Then he transformed back into his human form and said, "That's how I treat all my bitches that just won't let go."

"I am not a bitch," I cried. "I am Lana, your wife...your queen," I said to him as he walked away. "I am the mother of your pups, and I demand respect."

Gethambe continued to leave the room without acknowledging me. I sat there drenched in his urine when Samael reappeared.

"Well, that didn't go over well," he laughed. "Seems like things got a little pissy."

"What do you want?"

"Good news for you. The Gods are in your favor. You are too valuable to the pack, and you have not wronged your husband in any way. So, he can either step down and be with his half-breed, or he could remain king and be respectful, not loyal, to his wife. The decision is his to make."

"So, he will still be able to mingle with his human?"

"In a way. Per the Almighty, if he wants to continue a relationship with his half-breed, she has to be willing to live here with the other shape-shifters."

"So, she has shapeshifting abilities?" I inquired.

"Ashely has all types of abilities. She outranks you on power. She is gifted," he said. "Any who, deliver the message to your significant other, but I advise you to bathe first. And while you're at it, tell Gethambe to drink more water because his urine reeks," then he shimmered away.

I went to my chambers to clean the piss from my body, only to open the door and find Gethambe lying in our bed. I didn't have the energy to speak to him, and what did it matter if I did? He had become heartless and inconsiderate of my feelings. I was growing tired of this roller coaster ride that I was on with him.

So, I walked past our bed and made my way to the bathing chamber. I peeled out of my clothing and stepped into the hot springs. I allowed my body to become submerged into the water, trying to wash away his piss and my sins. Gethambe had won. He gets to have his cake and eat it too.

As I swam around the water, Gethambe appeared at the steps of the hot springs. He stood tall and was nude. He stepped down into the hot springs and swam over to me. I wasn't ready for another fight because I had no fight left in me. If he wanted Ashley so bad, he could have her.

"I was wrong," he apologized. "I shouldn't have peed on you. That was not right, and that is not the king I want to be."

I couldn't help but wonder if he had a chemical imbalance somewhere. One minute he's nice, and then the next minute, he's peeing on me. "Fighting is not good for the pups. I give up. You win, Gethambe. I just want to be happy and be a mother. If you want to give Ashley my crown, she can have it. Just let me walk away with our babies," I pleaded.

"Keep your crown. Together we will raise our pups.

They deserve to have a mother and father," he said, pulling me close to him. "I have to explain this situation to Ashley and allow her to make her own decision. If she decides to come here and join our pack, the crown will be split down the middle. I will love you both equally. There will be separate chambers, and I will divide my time between the two of you."

"And what brought about this change?" I asked him.

"Because I want to be a mirror image of my father. Perhaps even a greater king. And he would have never treated my mother the way I treated you. I apologize, Lana."

"Apology accepted."

"But keep in mind, I love Ashley. She holds my heart in her hands. I care for you. But I will try my best to make things work between the three of us. For the sake of this pack and my pups that you carry, I will try to work things out. In time, who knows, I may love you both equally," he said, pulling me to him and giving me a soft kiss.

We played in the water like old lovers. And he even took the time to help me wash myself, taking extra care as he washed my belly as he whispered sweet nothings to it.

"They will be here in about two and a half months," I said.

"I hope you have what you ask for. Two boys and one girl," he smiled.

"I pray that the Gods are listening."

"We are, but not all wishes come true," Samael said, shimmering into our bathing spa.

"A bit of privacy," Gethambe hissed at him.

Samael looked at him and shimmered away.

13

ASHLEY

I have been spending a lot of time with Gethambe lately, but something in my heart tells me he is hiding something from me. He seems to come around at the same time every day and can never stay the whole night. As soon as it begins to get dark, he has to leave. That makes me think that he is married. So, today I'm just going to ask him straight out. I don't have the time or patience to be someone's number two. Fuck that!

When I heard a knock at the door, I sprang to my feet and sprinted to it. I couldn't wait to see his face and let him hold me in his arms. I missed him. I flung the door open but was surprised that it wasn't Gethambe. Instead, it was Bullet. I hadn't seen him since the day that crap went down at the restaurant.

"Surprised to see me?" he smiled.

"Extremely," I replied, looking past him to see if Gethambe was anywhere close by. I didn't want to cause any problems between them.

"He's not here. He's at his compound with Lana," he said to me.

"Compound? Who's Lana?"

"There are some things you need to know, Ashley. And if you would allow me in, I will explain them to you."

I stood to the side and invited Bullet into my home, closing the door behind me. We walked into my living room, where I sat on the couch, and he sat in the chair across from me. Before he got into his story, I was already beginning to feel nauseated.

"So, what do I need to know?" I opened up the conversation.

"Gethambe is married. His wife's name is Lana. They were an arranged marriage, fated to be together since they were kids. They were married the night of the last full moon."

"He's married?" I questioned, with my heart falling into the pit of my stomach with pains shooting through my chest. "He's married?"

"Wait. There is more," he announced. "Remember that legend I was telling you about? The one with the wolves and mountain lions and how they are shape-shifters?" he asked. I had tears swelling in my eyes at the first set of news that he handed to me. Now he wanted me to recall an old legend he spoke about?

"Yes."

"Gethambe is a wolf, or as you would call him, a werewolf."

"What?" I asked in disbelief, thinking that Bullet was a little crazy. Why would he tell me that Gethambe was a wolf in sheep's clothing unless it was to benefit him in some way? Besides, there are no such things as werewolves. That is just something that you see in movies.

"I know you don't believe me, Ashley, but I'm telling you the truth."

"And I guess you are the mountain lion, his rival," I snapped.

"Yes. The mountain lions and wolves haven't gotten along for some years now. When our leader decided to switch sides, and the Gods punished our kind, we resented the wolves for not stepping up and taking us in. We could share these rich lands together, but they chose to be greedy and keep the fertile lands to themselves. Our leader may have betrayed the Gods, but the people remained loyal."

Okay. So, Bullet was the one who flew over the Cuckoo's nest and landed on his head. Because this story was fucking insane. I'm so glad I didn't end up falling for him. And it's a shame because he is so fucking gorgeous. From the long, black hair to his smooth and rich skin, all the way down his muscular physique, he was breathtaking.

"So, you're claiming to be a mountain lion?"

"No. I'm telling you I'm a mountain lion and that Gethambe is a wolf. I'm not making any false claims about being anything," he stated.

"Then let me see you in your mountain lion form," I said sarcastically. "Mr. Big Cat."

"Promise me that you won't run. When I transform, I am still me," he said, getting up from his seat and removing his clothes.

"Uhm, I said, transform into a mountain lion. Not give me a strip show," I laughed.

"I have to remove all my clothing because I can't wear them while I'm transforming, and if I transform with them on, my lion will rip them to shreds. And I don't want to walk out of your house naked," he smiled. "The women would attack me once they see all this dick."

So, I leaned back on my couch and watched him as he removed everything; his shirt, his pants, his socks, and then his boxers. And when I saw the monster dick he had been hiding in those pants, I had to gasp for air. That shit wasn't even hard, and it was huge as hell. When he walked over to me to place his clothes on the couch, it swung from side to side. Now he was truly blessed.

"I'm ready when you're ready," I said in disbelief.

He stood back and shook his body all over, relaxing his muscles. "Are you sure you're not going to run?" he asked.

"Positive."

As I stared at him, his face was the first thing that began to change. His ears grew upward as his face took on the look of a lion. I could hear his bones begin to crack as his body began to morph, right in front of me. His skin grew hair, turning a tawny color on the top and whitish underneath him. When he was fully transformed, his eyes were lined with a heavy black line, his fangs were long and pearly white, and his claws looked like knives.

I was in a total state of disbelief, mingled with a whole lot of fear. I was sitting in my living room with a predator, a skilled fucking killer. He was looking at me as if I was his next meal. I know I said I wouldn't run, and he didn't have to worry about that because I was too scared to anyway. I felt that if I moved, he would pounce on my back and rip my throat out. So, I did what any other woman would do; I sat there and yelled my fucking head off.

Then I heard as my door flung open and in came five wolves. They were snarling and salivating. All five were in an attack stance. The wolf that stood in the front was snow white and humongous. He was trailed by two gray wolves, a tawny brown one and a midnight black one. They were all equally scary. I had a fucking wildlife reserve in my living room, and I had no place to run.

Bullet slowly began to change back into his human form, and I ran into his arms. I wasn't sure if the wolf in the front was Gethambe or not, but I didn't want to take any chances if he wasn't.

"He won't hurt you," Bullet said, walking over to the couch to grab his clothes. "It's me he wants to kill."

"Don't leave me," I cried. "Take me with you," I begged, shaking uncontrollably.

Then Gethambe shifted into his mortal being. His face was stern and emotional. I could tell he was mad as hell, but at what, I didn't know.

Bullet pushed past him and the others, who followed him out of the front door. I was left standing in my living room looking at Gethambe, who was nude with his dick swinging. Today must have been my lucky day for big dicks.

"I didn't want you to find out this way," he said to me.

"What? That you're married? Or that I'm in love with a fucking animal? You know, people go to jail for this shit. It's called bestiality."

"Ashley, I didn't ask for this. I didn't ask for any of this. I was born with this gift, and so were my people."

"Gethambe, when did you plan on telling me that I was falling in love with a man who turns into a wolf? You have been coming around here for weeks, and now you want to spring this on me and think that I will be okay with it. Well, I'm not," I said. "And to top it off, Gethambe, you have a wife at home. Tell me — where would I fit in? If I could accept the fact that you are half man and half wolf, tell me where I would fit into a married man's life."

"Lana knows about us, and she accepts our union. I am the Alpha Male in my pack, the king of my society, and I would make you my queen," he said, his voice filled with sincerity.

"If you are a king, and you're married to Lana...wouldn't that make her your queen?"

I took the throw blanket from the couch and tossed it at him. The sight of his dick was making my pussy wet, and I wasn't anywhere close to getting over the fact that he was not all man.

He wrapped the blanket around his waist and sat down on the couch. I sat down beside him and put my face into my hands. I couldn't believe the shit I had just witnessed. Bullet was a fucking mountain lion, and Gethambe was a damn wolf. I knew all men were dogs, but I didn't think that people meant that literally.

"Let me show you my home," Gethambe said.

I looked at him in disbelief. He wanted to take me into a cave with a bunch of hungry ass wolves. I don't know what the hell he was thinking, but I'm no fool. And to meet his wife, he had to be crazy.

"I don't think I'm ready for all of that. As a matter of fact, I'm not even ready for the shit you just showed me."

"What are you saying to me?" he asked.

"Please leave," I said, with a single tear falling from my eyes. "I need space and some time to process all of this. Please, Gethambe, leave."

"Let me help you through this. There is so much you don't know that I could teach you."

All I could think about was his wife and how hard this had to be on her. I know how it feels to be cheated on. And I'm sure she didn't do anything to deserve this. And I know I couldn't live with myself if I continued seeing him now that I know about her.

"If you cared about me, you would leave. Give me the space that I ask for and need."

He pulled me into his arms and held me close to him. He gave me a couple of kisses on my forehead and then released his grip. He stood up and started for the door, taking a piece of me with him.

Gethambe didn't make it out of my door before I went into a full heartfelt cry. I thought I had found someone for me, only to find out he belonged to someone else. What have I done to deserve this?

I looked up at him with tears streaming from my eyes like a leaking faucet. I wanted desperately to beg him to come back to me, but I couldn't. He wasn't mine. He was Lana's.

Gethambe slammed the door closed and came rushing

back to me. I stood up to push him back, but he wrapped his arms around my waist and shoved his tongue into my mouth. At first, I tried to resist his advance, but he felt so good. This was more than a physical attraction; this was mental.

I wrapped my arms around his neck and gave into temptation. I could no longer resist the look of his strong masculine arms and his thick, musky scent. I pressed my lips to him, and we stood in the middle of my living room with our tongues locked in an emotional battle of desire. When he broke free, he looked into my eyes, losing his soul in mine. At that point, he had all of me, and he knew it. From the top of my head to the bottom of my feet – Gethambe had all of me.

He unbuttoned my shirt and slid it off my shoulders with the tip of his finger. The sight of my skin was enough to egg his growing erection on. I felt it throb against my leg as it began to grow and expand inside the confines of the throw blanket he had wrapped around him.

Gethambe slid his finger under the mid-section of my bra. When he had it in position, he extended his nail and cut the middle of my bra with one easy swipe. Proudly, my breasts stayed in place, sitting firm and high for him. His hands quickly covered my breasts and twiddled my nipples between his rough, thick fingers.

"Mmmh," I moaned, laying my head on his chest, as I enjoyed the sensation of him playing aggressively with my taut nipples.

"I want you, but I'm not sure if I should try to enter

your body," he whispered to me. "When I get aroused, my beast tends to rear its ugly face."

"I want you to," I answered, barely able to breathe from the excitement.

"We can try, and I'm going to go slow, but if I get too rough...stop me," he directed.

"Okay," I murmured. Then he picked me up and cradled my body in his firm, muscular arms. He carried me to my room and pulled back the plush white comforter I had on my bed.

"White isn't the best color for this night," he laughed, laying me down on the bed. Then he removed the throw blanket that he had wrapped around his waist.

When I saw his dick, I gulped. I mean, I loved a big dick, but *that* was ungodly. There was no way in hell he was going to be able to fit all that in me. At least, not without him tearing me apart.

"I'm scared," I confessed, my lips trembling.

"Don't be," he said; his voice was so calm and soothing.

I removed the ripped bra and tossed it to the side. I lifted my body slightly and removed my panties and jeans simultaneously, throwing them onto the floor. Then I laid there stiffly, anxiously waiting for him to make his next move.

He stood over me quietly, admiring my body. As he licked his lips, I saw his teeth grow in length.

"While I'm intimate with you, there are going to be some changes with my body. When they happen, don't be scared, it's normal," he advised.

"Okay," I said, mentally bracing myself for what was to come.

I watched him stroke his dick slowly as it continued to grow. Then he climbed into the bed and pushed my legs open, exposing my sacred garden. He dipped his head down between my thighs and began to sniff and lick my nub passionately. Gethambe nibbled, sucked, and slobbered over my lips, eagerly kissing me from my asshole to my clit. When he came up for air, his face was covered in my cream, and his eyes were a fiery red. My heartbeat quickened, but it was with excitement, not fear.

He lowered his head again and sucked the cream that leaked steadily from my wetness. He rolled his tongue in circles as he smothered my pussy with his lustful love. I slowly rotated my hips, riding his tongue like a bicycle, paddling my way to heaven.

"*Mmmmh*," I moaned, "Don't stop, Daddy,"

He continued to bathe my lady with his tongue until I erupted in sheer pleasure. My body was trembling, and ecstasy overcame me. My hands dug into the sheets as I arched my back and moaned. This fueled him to continue bathing my clit, passionately. When he drank all that I had to offer, he snaked his long, velvet tongue inside of me in search of more.

When he was finished, he sat up on his knees and howled. His voice was loud and deafening. Suddenly, I heard his pack join in, but they were quieter as if they were miles away. The ones that escorted him to me howled in unity, loud enough to make my windows vibrate.

He looked down at me as he wiped his mouth with the

back of his hand. Then he came down on top of me, and I could see his eyes clearly now. They were still red as fire, but his face was soft and inviting. His fangs protruded from his mouth; they were long, sharp, and pearly white. I lifted my head and began to suck on one and then the other. I pulled his bottom lip into my mouth, biting on it gently. He growled an intimate growl, making me smile slightly.

"Are you ready?" he asked softly.

"Yes," I answered.

"Tell me if you need me to stop," he directed.

Then he grabbed his dick and teased the length of my opening with its head. Slowly, he began to push inside of me. It was intensely painful. I felt as if he was ripping me apart, shredding my sacred place. But I relented and allowed him to keep pushing into me as I wiggled my hips to ease his entrance.

"FUCK!" he yelled, "What are you doing?"

I curled my arms around his neck and pulled him closer to me. Slowly, gritting through the pain, I begin to grind on the half of him that he had inside of me.

"Ssshh, Baby," I whispered. "Let me work the rest of it in," I said, gently running my fingers through his hair.

He nodded in agreement with his eyes shut tightly. His body jerked slightly as I eased him in gracefully, an inch at a time. Little by little, I felt him fill me. He huffed, grunted, and moaned as I continued to swirl my hips and indulge in his abnormally large package with care and patience.

I could feel his body warm, but he didn't perspire. I, on the other hand, was pouring with sweat under this massive beast. I was steaming, drenched, and began to feel tired.

Ready for him to take the lead, I gave him an indicative kiss as the go-ahead to make love to me.

"Are you sure?" he asked again. "Everything is going great, and I don't want to hurt you." I could see that his eyes were filled with concern.

"I'm sure. It will be okay."

Slowly, he began to thrust into me. Immediately, I reconsidered my choice. Even the slightest, gentlest thrust felt like a heavy, thumping pounding. He was supporting his weight on one elbow as he glided in and out of me. I felt myself scooting backward, trying to pull away from his swift, hammering strokes, but when he noticed, he huffed and pulled me back to him.

"Don't run," he whispered. "It triggers my instincts, making me want to chase my prey," he warned. "If you need me to stop, just tell me."

"No," I whispered, panting, refusing to give in to the pain.

He began to thrust into me again, this time a little harder and a little quicker. I couldn't breathe; my heart was pounding viscously against my chest. Slowly, an over-whelming pleasure emanated through my body; his dick sent shockwaves of immense, unbridled ecstasy. As he continued to push into me, I climaxed several times, impaled on his long, girthy spear.

"G-Gethhambbe," I cried out. "Fuck me harder! Fuck me!" I yelled, enjoying all of him.

He was now delving deep into me and pounding fiercely. Even with the amazing sensations that I was indulging in, the sharp pain that came with his thrusts remained. Again, without realizing it, I scooted back and tried to ease the pressure.

This time, there was no warning. His claws unsheathed, his eyes burned redder than they had before, and his howl deepened. He yanked my body back down under him, pinning me as he began to power thrust into my core. His balls were slapping against my ass, his hardness filling me completely, as his claws dug into my thigh and shoulder.

"Stop! Stop!" I cried though a part of me wanted him to ignore my pleas.

"It's too late," he growled. "My dick has to release," he said, struggling to speak between his deep, guttural growls.

He thrusted, he pounded, he dug his nails deeper into my skin, and then he took my neck into his mouth and began sucking.

I arched my back and brought my body up to meet his. My breasts pressed into his broad chest as I wrapped my legs around his waist and rode his swift strokes eagerly. I wanted to feel as much of his thick, animalistic dick inside me as I possibly could.

"I'm cumming!" I cried out, feeling the waves of elation rush through me while falling quickly into euphoria.

Gethambe howled again, and his pack howled in unison with him. I could tell from his howl and the twisted look on his face that it was his turn to cum. His volcano erupted deep into my core, and as my body shuddered in gratification, I felt him buck and jerk while spurts of his cum filled me to the hilt.

When he was done, he collapsed onto my body. I could still feel his hardness as it twitched uncontrollably.

"I can't pull out until it goes down," he told me.

"Okay," I whispered, playing in his long, silky, black hair.

We lay there for about an hour, just holding each other while his hardness softened. I held him tightly, and he held me. I was in love with him. I knew I was wrong for sleeping with a married man, but I love him.

"Where do we go from here?" I asked him.

"I want you to come home with me," he answered. "Meet Lana and become my wife."

"I don't know if I want to share you."

"I won't share you," he said. "I want all of you or none of you."

"But you're asking me to share you with another woman?"

"She's carrying my pups. I was promised to her before we were even born. The Gods arranged our marriage. We had no control over it," he explained. I could hear the sorrow in his voice as he told me about Lana.

"And she's pregnant?" I asked, with tears swelling in my eyes.

"Yes. The pups will be here soon. We can raise them together. This way of life is not uncommon. I will marry you and provide for all your needs. I just need to hear you say, '*yes*.'"

I could have pondered, but I knew my answer already.

"Yes. I will marry you and become your second wife. I will love your children as if they were my own," I promised him. "But only with the blessing of your first wife and your parents."

"Then pack your things; I will be back to get you in a week. I need to get things together for your arrival, and I have to send for my parents," he said, slowly pulling out of me.

"So, I won't see you for a whole week?"

"It may take me two weeks. I have to meet with the elders, and my parents don't live in this world. I want to make sure that everything is just right for your arrival. But my crew will be around here to check on you daily. I promise I will be back for you."

"I know you will," I said, kissing him softly. He got out of the bed and checked the sheets.

"I need to change your bedding. It's bloody."

I looked down and noticed that I was lying in a pool of blood. As morbid as it was, it looked like I had had another miscarriage.

"Do I need to go to the hospital?" I asked, concerned.

"No. It's normal because of my size. But you handled it well," he laughed.

"Go ahead and go handle your business; I'll get this cleaned up," I told him.

He pulled me to him and gave me a long, sensual kiss. Surprisingly, I could sense him revving up for a second round. Succumbing to his desires, he knelt at the edge of the bed and rubbed his nose in my pussy, his tongue gently separating my lips.

I backed away and told him to go. God knew I couldn't take a second round with that beast, at least not right now. I had some serious healing to do.

Gethambe stood and kissed me one final time before leaving.

"I love you," I said to him.

"I love you more," he replied and disappeared.

I made sure all my doors were locked and changed my bed. I hopped in and nestled my body deep beneath the sheets and fell quickly to sleep. Dreaming of the man I was soon to marry.

14

GETHAMBE

I was in a joyful mood when my parents and the elders arrived for a meeting of the minds. I felt they would agree with me having a second wife because they didn't really care about recycling a life. They wanted all of us to move through this life in one try, although some of their actions may show differently. But I just chalked it up to them being petty like that.

Lana was flying on cloud nine by the time they had arrived. I knew how important it was to have her on my side, so I did what I needed to do and rocked her *beast-loving world*. I took her to the hot springs and bathed her body with sweet-smelling herbs and spices. I dried her body and kissed her belly, telling my pups that their father loved them. I carried her to our bed and gave her a sensual massage, and then I licked and sucked at her sweetness, giving her multiple orgasms.

I made her howl in delightful ecstasy as I passionately tortured her body. By the time I was finished with Lana, her legs had shaken uncontrollably, and she was sucking her thumb like a newborn human baby. I knew my boundaries with her, so I didn't insert my hardness into her body, but I fingered her wetness and tasted her juices until her well ran dry.

As I sat at the head of the table with Lana on my right side, I began to plead my case to bring Ashley into our society.

"I have called this meeting because I wanted to ask for your approval to marry Ashley. I understand that this is not typical, but I'm deeply in love with her and addicted to her being. I have gotten the approval of my wife, who is willing to accept her into our family, but Lana will reign as First Queen."

"What type of trickery is this?" Pax asked. Lana's father was a strong man and fiercely loyal to the traditions of our society.

"This doesn't happen in our society. Only whores and savages have multiple partners!" Cherish spat, giving me the evil eye. I couldn't even believe she would be upset; she never really cared for her daughter. The whole time they were here in this realm, she cared more about her designer clothes and trips into the inner city than she had ever cared about her children.

"Watch your tongue!" my father warned. "He is not only the king, but he's my son, you selfish bitch! I will cut your tongue from your mouth and have you lick your own ass if you become disrespectful towards him again!"

"My apologies for her mouth, Elder King," Pax said, bowing his head to my father. Although he was loyal to tradition, he was more devoted to my father.

"Arguments and disagreements," Samael announced nonchalantly, as his wives giggled.

"Stupid woman...Samael has four wives; does this make him a savage?" Lilith questioned, looking at Lana mysteriously. I was a little confused because Lana wasn't the one who commented; it was her mother. But as Lilith gazed upon Lana, her eyes glowed emerald-green with hints of canary yellow. And before I knew it, all the wives were looking at her mysteriously.

"And what are your thoughts, young queen?" Samael questioned.

"I stand behind my husband. It would be nice to have a sister-wife to help me take care of these pups and spend the long and lonely days with while Gethambe is away," Lana answered.

I looked at the wives as they were studying her every word and noticed that Lilith's eyes now glowed the most beautiful shade of ruby red, but her skin became white as snow. She appeared to be sickened by my wife's willingness to accept Ashley into our lives.

"Ebonee, would you like to add your input?" Samael asked.

"I support my son and approve of his decision. I feel that it is a just one. Instead of sending Lana through reincarnation, he is allowing her to live out this life as a queen and rule beside him," she stated. "My only concern is, how much power would be given to the second wife, and will it cause conflict within the den?"

"They will be equal. Yes, Lana will be known as the first wife, and her opinion on any situation will be valuable, but the second wife's opinion will be heard and respected with just as much authority as the first wife," Samael answered.

Then he placed his hands on the table, and his body illuminated the room with a bright gold tint. His eyes turned white, and the room was engulfed in a smothering state of tranquility as he began to foretell the future:

A decision from the first wife will cause great chaos within these walls. Because of this decision, a war will be on the horizon, and the king will lose many men to make right her wrongs. I see a great sadness and death.

Ashley will rise and bring about peace, but not in the way you think. She is way more powerful than you know and will use that power to unite the mountain lions and the wolves. During this pack's darkest days, she will be valuable, whereas the young queen's power shall dwindle away.

It all boils down to the decision of the first wife. Choose your destiny wisely.

Then the gold tint disappeared, and Samael looked at Lana along with his wives.

"What does that even mean?" Lana cried out. "Stop talking in riddles, and just tell me how to fix it!"

"I cannot make that choice for you. I can only tell you that you have a great decision to make, and it can either hinder this pack's progress or elevate it," Samael explained. "I am only a messenger of the Almighty. He only gives me clips of what is to come. But as I warned you before, one small thing can make a massive impact in your future days."

Lana's parents ate in silence along with mine. The wives of Samael talked to each other in secret, glancing in

Lana's direction from time to time. I had an odd feeling that they knew more about Samael's vision than they wanted us to know. And whatever it was, I could see them distancing themselves from Lana.

"I will go in town and retrieve Ashley today. I have made all the preparations to make her stay here comfortable. I believe that she has no clue about her powers, so I will leave that to you, Samael, to inform her and to show her the way," I said.

"No need. Once she enters these walls, her powers will be awakened. I researched her background and found that she is a direct descendant of the Almighty's bloodline. Her blood is his blood. Her family is a part of the original bloodline linked between Heaven and Hell. I knew that she was filled with old magic, but I didn't realize how old her heritage was until I dug deep into her tree of life."

"What are you hiding about this human?" my father wanted to know.

"Oh, poor Elder King," Samael laughed. "Gethambe's new wife-to-be isn't human at all."

"Not human at all?" Cherish asked; her voice was soft but slightly elevated.

"Nooooo. Ashley is a descendant of the Charmeine, the angel of harmony; a descendant of the Archangel Michael, the angel of loyalty, and I have found that she has the blood of Lilith, the first succubus, flowing through her veins. Once she realizes the powers that her essence harbors, Ashley will become a force to be reckoned with. However, if Gethambe doesn't tie the knot with that vivacious creature and he allows her to slip through his fingers, the mountain lions will benefit greatly from her abilities," Samael explained.

"Bullet just arrived at Ashley's home, and she invited him inside of her domicile," I heard Rouge say to me telepathically.

"He's on his way," Lana answered, looking at me with fear in her eyes. "Go get her and bring her here to her new home. I will get everything together; you will wed her *today*," she said aloud.

"Wise choice, young queen," Samael said, nodding his head, with his wives following his lead. But Lilith's eyes remained reddened as she gazed upon Lana. I'm sure that she had known long before my chance meeting with Ashley that she was her descendant. Legend stated that one of the children Lilith gave birth to survived her curse for leaving the Garden of Eden. Although it was said that Lilith never had the chance to care for that child, she knew her daughter was hidden here on Earth. She was not able to locate her because the Almighty cloaked her location from all the Gods.

Pax and my father rose as I did and offered their assistance in obtaining Ashley to ensure her safety on the journey here to Achaemenid. Lana slowly rose to her feet and started for the chapel to hurry along the arrangements for the wedding but fell to her knees in excruciating pain. My pups were knocking on the door of life and were ready to enter this world.

"UHG!" she yelled. "They're coming," she cried.

Cherish and my mother ran to her side with the aid of Na'amah and Eisheth Zenunim. They helped her to her feet and assisted her to our chambers to prepare her body for birthing.

"Don't worry, Gethambe. They have a lot of experience in delivering children. She will be in great hands," Samael advised. "Go and get your second wife and soulmate."

"We will make the preparations for a wedding," Lilith announced as I watched her eyes turn a calming color of sage. As soon as Lana was removed from her presence, she became that same old playful, seductive demon that I had known all my life.

My father, Pax, and I all morphed into our beasts and ran with lightning speed toward Ashley's home to meet up with the others.

"I don't know what is going on, but they are getting into her car. I'm sure I heard Bullet say the word casino." Rouge reported.

"When I was near a window, I heard him talking to her about the old prophecies. But he didn't want to stay at her house too long because her home sat in between their land and ours." Juice said.

"Does she know you guys are there?" I questioned.

"Yes. I made my presence known to her earlier this morning. She even offered me something to eat, but I had just fed on a juicy, young rabbit." Joker snickered.

"I've heard from everyone but Stewart. Where is he?" I questioned.

"Following the car but keeping enough distance from them to keep Bullet from picking up my scent." He chimed in.

"Are they going toward our casino?" I asked.

"*Yes,*" he answered.

"*Good. Stay with them. Everyone else head in that direction because the lions run in packs around there. I am with the Elder King and Pax, so we should have no problem defending ourselves or Ashley,*" I directed.

"*Juice, since you are the closest to them now, once you arrive at the casino, go to the security room and notify the Canine Crew that works there of the situation. They would know how to prepare for whatever may happen,*" Pax stated. These were men that were personally trained by him, extremely loyal to our pack and traditions.

"*We haven't fought side by side in years, my old friend,*" my father said, looking over at his long-time friend as we ran together as a pack.

"*Well, I'm hoping neither one of you old motherfuckers break a hip during battle,*" I said, making the elders laugh.

As we approached the casino, we all morphed into human form and went through the secret entrance. We found clothes there for any pack member to wear just in case something like this happened.

I looked at my father as he dressed and then at Pax and laughed at them. "How in the hell did you two old bastards keep your wives happy with that little shit?"

"Boy, I was so deep in your birth canal that your mother was throwing up the head of my dick for weeks," my father joked.

"And I've never had any complaints from Cherish or any of your many chambermaids that I had the pleasure of dicking down," Pax laughed.

We dressed quickly and rushed up to the main floor. As

soon as we made it to the lobby, we were all captivated by her alluring aroma. It was so intoxicating that I could feel my dick grow with want. I licked my lips and could taste her sweetness as if she was lying in bed, allowing me to lick her dry.

"Jesus Christ!" Pax said, elevating his voice slightly. "Is she in heat or something?"

"It is stronger than usual," I explained. "With the variety of blood that she has running in her veins...I'm not sure if she has a heat cycle or if this is just normal."

"Well, if she is in heat, we need to make haste and get her into a secure location before your rival gets lucky tonight. And we all know that she must be a very sexual creature if she has Lilith's blood coursing through hers," my father stated.

We proceeded to the casino, which was jam-packed with humans as well as mountain lions. I was hoping like hell that we weren't going to have to make a scene, but my gut feeling said that I was in for the fight of my life.

I saw Ashley sitting at the bar with Bullet. They seemed to be in a deep, sensual conversation. I noticed that her body was leaning in towards him, and she was laughing at something he said. My blood was boiling, and my temper was instantly intensified. I was so damn mad that I couldn't think straight.

I walked over to her with my posse behind me, grabbed the glass from her hand, and slammed it down onto the bar, shattering it into a million pieces. I looked at a stunned Ashley and asked, "What part of I don't share what's mine with anyone, don't you understand?"

"We were just out having a drink and talking about legends of the past," she answered calmly.

"Get your shit, and let's go," I demanded.

Bullet stood up and faced me. I could tell that tonight, he was ready for a fight. It wasn't like when we faced off in the restaurant, and I easily took Ashley from him. No, this was different. His whole demeanor had changed, and he had found his courage.

"Not tonight nigga," he said. His voice was firm and cold.

"Bullet," I said calmly. "You're going to fuck around, and fuck around, and tickle me...bitch boy. You might want to practice on some of your friends before you fuck with an Alpha Male like me," I laughed in his face.

"The amphitheater?" he questioned. "You and me, my nigga. Winner takes Ashley."

"Hold up now. I'm sitting right here and can make my own choices," she said, standing up and positioning her body between us.

"Ain't no winner takes all here. I've already mated with her and laid the foundation for a life of eternity with her. She has already accepted my marriage proposal," I said, chuckling. I didn't need the promise of being with Ashley to kill him, but I loved the invitation to a fight.

"Look. We are drawing the attention of the humans," Rouge said. "Are we about to tear this motherfucker up or walk away and let them live to fight another day?" Rouge was smooth with his words. I have never seen him mad or upset about anything. Even when he was ready to knuckle up, his emotions were untouched.

"If you want to handle this at the arena, we can. I don't have bitch running through my veins; I fear no man, mortal or immortal," I announced, welcoming the challenge.

"There will be no amphitheater. There will be no fighting. And I'm not something that you can just toss around like a prize. I made my choice to marry you, become your second wife, and I am standing behind that."

"Ashley, dear heart, it's time for us to go before this situation gets out of hand and a bunch of people die," Jabari, my father, advised her. "I know that you may not have meant any harm, but there is a lot of bad blood between the two tribes."

"She's not going any –"

Before Bullet could finish his sentence, I planted my fist into his cheek. I struck him with so much power that it tossed him into the bar, and blood came pouring out of his mouth. He tried to brace himself for the impact, but the force of my blow was too strong.

I could sense his pride coming toward us, but he held up one hand, and they stopped dead in their steps. He wiped the blood from his mouth and looked at me. "I respect the people here too much to cause them any harm. If you would like to continue this fight to see who the better fighter is, we can meet at the arena."

Ashley ran to his side, grabbed a napkin from the bar, and assisted him in wiping the blood away. I started toward him again to be pulled back by Pax and my father.

"He's right, my son. This isn't the place for this. These people would not understand what we are," he explained.

I watched as she gently wiped the blood away, dabbing

it in a glass of water and cleaning his wound tenderly, with love and care. I could see the sorrow in her eyes as she looked at him and the hostility as she looked at me.

"I'm so sorry for this," Ashley apologized to Bullet. "If I knew this would have happened, I wouldn't have ever suggested that we hang out for a little while."

"Never be sorry, my sweet Ash. I knew this was going to happen, it's my destiny and yours," he smiled at her, running his finger down the contour of her face.

I became enraged with jealousy and pulled her to me. "You have a wedding to attend," I announced, loud enough for Bullet to catch my drift.

"You shouldn't have to stand for being someone's number two," Bullet replied with sarcasm covering his words. "Someone as special as you are should only be considered a number one, a first wife, and a top priority."

I understood what he was saying weighed heavy on her heart, but my love for her was strong, and her love for me was even more potent. What we shared could not be broken, not even by a smooth-talking lion.

I put my hand in the small of her back and led her to the front door, where Joker had several cars waiting for us. We could only drive so far, and then we would have to morph into our beasts and run the remainder of the way. Since Ashley's powers hadn't awakened, I had decided that I would carry her through the mountains to our secure location.

As we drove in silence, I held her close to me and inhaled her sweet, irresistible scent. It was so powerful that all who were around her were ready to mate. She was exciting not only me but also any male wolf within fifty miles of our location. We could hear the howls of lust as it floated on the wind.

When we made it to a small cabin near our den, I advised her that when I morphed into my beast, she was to climb on my back, and I would carry her the rest of the way. It had become dark, and I was worried about carrying her through these treacherous terrains, knowing that Bullet's people were always ready to mount an attack on our people. But I knew that Bullet had developed some deep-rooted feelings for Ashley and hoped this would be a reason for him to call his pack off, just this one time.

We made it to the gates of our den. As we approached it, Achaemenid illuminated. Ashley climbed down from my back, and we all morphed into our human form as we made our way through the large golden gates.

She looked at all the naked men behind her and began to giggle like a schoolgirl. God, she was so beautiful, so kind, and all mines. I loved her so much and couldn't wait to officially tie her down to keep any other man or beast from possessing her sweetness. She was the crack to my pipe, and I was addicted to her aura, her being.

With her first step into the golden gates, the necklace that she wore glowed gold, then white, and then nothing. Her hair blew wildly, but there was no wind, and her eyes turned the color of soft baby blue. I believe her inner strength was being awakened.

As we approached Lilith and Agrat bat Mahlat, they instantly bowed to her. This was something that I had never seen the elder wives do for anyone. They were above us. As we moved toward the dining hall, Samael appeared. He, too, bowed at the sight of Ashley. I didn't know if they were doing this out of respect or if Ashley's mixed blood afforded her a position of royalty among our kind.

"Your children have not made it into this world. They are causing Lana a lot of pain and heartache. She cries out for you, and I think it would be best if you go to her and let her know that you have made it home safe and sound," Samael directed. "And the rest of you...go put on some clothes and quit acting like savages."

"I'm not sure if I should leave Ashley in your charge," I snapped.

"I promise to keep her safe. Besides, she won't be with me. Lilith and Agrat bat Mahlat will get her prepared for the wedding that must take place tonight. This will be the last full moon of the year. Nuptial ceremonies can only take place during that time. And hopefully, a child would be conceived to satisfy my wife, Lilith."

"Go, foolish boy king. She is of my blood, and no harm will come to her," Lilith agreed.

I kissed Ashley on her forehead and told her to be strong. "I will only be gone for a moment. Just long enough to check on Lana and my pups. Once I know that she is okay, I will be right back here to take your hand in marriage. The elders will take care of you and explain our ritual," I explained.

"I'm not scared," she answered. "I feel like I am finally home."

We exchanged a short, passionate kiss, and then I made my way to my chambers to console my first wife, who was giving birth to our pups. I was followed by Pax, my father, Rouge, Joker, Stewart, and Juice. Because birth is a celebration, the father is accompanied by his closest friends and family.

I hated leaving Ashley in a room of conniving demons, but I didn't have a choice.

15

LANA

I had been waiting for hours for my husband to come and be with me while I delivered his pups. These babies are refusing to leave my womb and grace this world with their presence. Instead, they want to stay where they know they're safe from the evils of this world.

"Ugh," I yelled out as another contraction started.

"Breathe," my mother said, wiping the sweat from my head.

"Where is my husband?" I cried.

"He has just arrived. He's on his way here as we speak," Ebonee answered.

I could see Na'amah and her sidekick Eisheth Zenunim looking at my sacred garden and whispering to each other. I could feel that something wasn't right, but I couldn't understand what they were saying. Besides, they were speaking in the old language, Aramaic. They spoke it with a dialect that was almost impossible for me to translate, and I knew that they were doing it on purpose.

"Is there something wrong with my pups?" I questioned.

"Besides, they won't come out? No," Eisheth Zenunim laughed.

"I'm sorry if I don't find your elder jokes funny. I need to know if my babies are going to be okay?" I pleaded.

"Only the Almighty can answer that," Cherish answered.

"Or Samael," I said. "He has the gift of sight and can tell me if my children will make it into this world. Usually, pups are born within an hour or so of the mother going into labor. What is going on right now isn't normal," I explained, although everyone in the room knew that already.

"Uhhh," I cried out again. This time I could hear my chamber room door open. I looked over in that direction and saw the one person that lit my entire world up, Gethambe.

"I'm here, Lana. I'm here to help you through this," he said, racing to the side of the bed.

He crawled in the bed beside me and began to lick my face. He stroked the side of my stomach, giving me some relief from the pain. Being this close to him and wrapped in his arms, I felt safe, and I felt like our children were safe.

"How many are there?" he asked.

"As far as I can tell, at least four," Na'amah advised him. Hearing her answer Gethambe with a compassionate and understanding voice made my blood boil with hatred. The whole time they have been here, they have barely opened their mouths to give me any news. I've only heard them repeat those irritating statements, "stupid queen," "foolish queen," "young queen," and "they will come when they're ready." But when Gethambe asks them a question, they answer him politely and respectfully.

"What is taking them so long to come?" he asked them.

"They're refusing to turn and descend into her pelvis," Eisheth Zenunim answered.

"Can't you reach inside of her womb and turn them?" my mother, Cherish, asked.

"We could, but there is a chance that not all the pups will survive the transition or if any of them will make it. Turning them while they are in the womb is not only difficult on the pups, but it will be difficult on Lana as well," Samael said, shimmering into our chambers.

"So, do we wait it out?" Ebonee asked.

"If you wait much longer, the pups and their mother will certainly die. If they reach in and turn the pups and pull them down, the pups may die. This is a choice for the young queen and Gethambe to make," he answered.

Gethambe looked at me, waiting for me to make a decision. I wanted to be here with him, with our children. I wasn't ready to die, but I didn't want to lose the life of any of my pups.

"I don't want to lose you," Gethambe said, stroking my hair. I honestly believed him; his eyes displayed his sincerity.

"But you will be able to live out your life with Ashley," I said, with one tear falling from my eye.

"Don't talk like that," he said. "I do love Ashley, that I cannot deny. But I love the mother of my children as well, and we were promised to each other at birth. Even with

Ashley holding the keys to my heart, she only holds the keys to half of it. Lana, you complete it," he told me.

"If they turn them, some of our pups may not make the journey into this world," I warned him.

"I'd rather have many years with you than to live many years without you. We can have more children if you decide to go forward with allowing the elders to proceed and save those that we can save, and give the Almighty the ones we cannot," Gethambe said.

I didn't want to sacrifice one for the lives of three, but I didn't want to die a young queen before I reigned. This was the hardest decision of my life, and I was having an internal battle with myself trying to rationalize which decision would be best.

"Uhhhhhhg," I yelled.

"You need to make a decision quickly, young queen, before you all die," Samael warned.

"Turn them," I whispered. "Turn them and try to save them all."

With that, Na'amah grabbed some warm towels and a pale of warm water from the hot springs. She ordered that my mother hold one leg up and open as Ebonee did the same. "Gethambe, when I tell you to, help her push by pushing on her stomach," she instructed.

Eisheth Zenunim and Na'amah fooled around between my legs for several seconds, and I could feel a lot of pressure.

"Lana, it is important that you lie perfectly still while I reach inside of your womb and turn the first pup. It's going to feel uncomfortable and maybe even painful, but try your best not to move," Na'amah warned.

"Okay," I answered, trying to deep breathe through the contractions and the pain.

I could feel as she entered my womb. There was a lot of pushing and pulling, and I could swear I could feel the pup's claws tearing my insides apart. The pain was almost unbearable, but I refused to move. What were only minutes felt like hours.

"Gethambe, push down gently on Lana's stomach. Lana push," Na'amah directed.

As I pushed, I could feel my pup pass through my cervix and heard its voice as it entered this world. Eisheth Zenunim grabbed the pup and began cleaning it, and handed it off to the chambermaid.

We continued the steps over and over until all the pups were out. I didn't hear them all cry, but I was sure that I heard two of them. If two pups made it out of four, I was okay with that. Yes, I am devastated that I have lost my children's lives, but I was still here and sharing my life with the love of my life.

"How many?" Gethambe asked.

"There were five," Na'amah answered. "One survived."

"Nooooooo!" I yelled. "Why are my life and body cursed?" I cried.

"It's okay," my mother said. "Don't cry. It's okay," she repeated.

"Do I have a son or daughter?" Gethambe asked. The first-born son would become the future king. Any son born after that would serve other important roles of this society. I wanted to be the one to give him his first son, not Ashley. If she were to bless him with a son before I did, our roles would be reversed, and she would become the first wife, and I would become the second wife.

"You are the father of a healthy baby girl," Eisheth Zenunim announced. My heart sank deep into my stomach with regret. I wouldn't be able to have another litter for six months, but Ashley would be able to get pregnant right away. I just couldn't allow her to give Gethambe his first son, no matter the cost.

Eisheth Zenunim brought our daughter to us. She was wrapped in a soft blanket and smelled of a new baby. I refused to hold her. I didn't even want to see her, so I turned my head to avoid the sight of our daughter.

So, Eisheth Zenunim gave Gethambe his daughter as she assisted Na'amah with the pups that didn't make it.

"Which one was the first to come out?" I had to know.

"Your son," Na'amah answered. "You were blessed with four sons and one daughter. Only your daughter survived."

"And what a pretty girl she is," Gethambe praised. My mother, Ebonee, Samael, and Gethambe's personal crew gathered around the bed to see his daughter. He passed her around the room, allowing everyone to hold and kiss her. When she made her way back to me, I refused to look at her or accept her into my arms.

"Lana," Gethambe said. He was looking at me with concern in her eyes. There was no way I could explain to him how I detested his daughter and how I wished she was the one to die instead of my sons. No matter how much I wanted to bond with her, I couldn't.

"Take it away," I demanded. "Get that monster away from me."

"Lana," Gethambe said again. "This is our daughter. Why would you call her a monster?"

"Because that beast killed our sons, Gethambe!"

"She had nothing to do with that, Lana. She's an innocent baby," he tried to explain to me. I didn't want to hear any excuses, and I didn't want anything to do with the baby. I refused to hold her, and I refused to look at her.

"Clear my room!" Gethambe yelled. "Mother, take my daughter with you."

As they made haste getting out of our chambers, I knew that I would have to stand my ground and not give in to his childish demands. Gethambe could not force me to bond with a child I wanted nothing to do with for all the love in his heart.

"I don't have much to say to you. But what little words I have for you, I advise that you hear every word. Either you pull your shit together and become a mother to our daughter and a wife to me, or I will easily move Ashley into your place. I'm sure that she would be more than willing to be a first wife and a mother to my daughter. The decision is yours to make, and you only have until tomorrow to make it."

"And if I don't?" I asked. "What if I don't give you what you want, Gethambe? You're going to threaten me with reincarnation?" I snapped.

"No. I'm going to snap your neck and move forward with a happy life with Ashley. I won't give you the pleasure of a second chance at life," he threatened me.

"Then snap my fucking neck and condemn my soul to hell. I don't give two fucks. I will never accept her as mine, and I would never act motherly towards her," I advised him. "Please leave me and go marry the woman you truly love."

He looked at me and stormed out of my chambers. I heard him tell the guards that nobody was allowed into my room, and I wasn't allowed out. He told them that food wasn't even to be given to me unless he approved the delivery himself.

I have just been imprisoned in my room. And to add salt to my wounds, all four of my dead sons were left in the room with me. I was told that I needed to get out of the bed, wash their tiny bodies, and wrap them in a spice-dipped cloth to prepare them for their royal funeral. I knew that Gethambe would not allow me to attend because I wasn't willing to accept our daughter's life.

I had no energy to perform the job I had been tasked with, but I had to get it done soon. They would be here in the morning to take them away. To say a prayer over them and give them back to the Almighty.

Lilith and Agrat bat Mahlat have been so attentive to my needs. They have waited on me hand and foot to prepare me for this wedding. Although I was able to bathe myself, they insisted on helping me. Lilith stepped into the tub with me with Agrat bat Mahlat and together, they washed me from the top of my head to the bottom of my feet. Lilith took extra care as she ran the sponge over my belly.

"You will give Gethambe many babies," she whispered. I was amazed by her unmatched beauty. She looked as if she could be Asian, but she also looked as if she could be black. She was slender and elegant, but her English wasn't the greatest. Whatever accent she had, it was heavy but understandable, to a degree.

"Can you see the future?" I asked her.

"No," she laughed. "I can only see if you have viable seeds for fertilizing," she explained.

"You need to explain to her our traditions," Agrat bat Mahlat said.

"Ashley, you are going to go through a lot this night. When Gethambe takes you to be his second wife, it is not acknowledged as a union until you consummate your marriage. And the act will be done in your chambers in front of his parents, all the elders, and the spirits of your parents that Anubis himself will summon," Lilith explained.

"I will get to see my mother and father again?" I asked her.

"Only their spirit. They have already crossed over to the other side. They will be able to see you, but you will not be able to communicate with them. Once Gethambe enters your body as your husband, Anubis will take them back to their Heavenly home," she answered.

"I'm not afraid," I told Lilith.

"I know you're not. I can sense your strength," she assured me. Lilith stepped out of the tub first and held her hand out for me to follow her. I reached up and grabbed her hand and followed her to a bench where I sat looking into a mirror at my nude body.

Agrat bat Mahlat rushed over to where I sat and began to dry my body as Lilith stood behind me, combing through my hair. I don't know why I wasn't uncomfortable with two naked women catering to me, but I wasn't; it just felt normal. I didn't have to do anything for myself. I didn't have to wash my body, apply the lotions or perfumes, and I didn't have to dress myself. They did it all for me.

"When will I become pregnant?" I asked.

"Tonight. But this fertilized egg is not yours to keep. The first child is given to me as a sacrifice for the many powers that we give you in return. A long time ago, I refused to submit to my husband, and I left the Garden of Eden to find happiness. Not long after I left, I was rescued by my knight in shining armor. But my punishment for being disobedient to the Almighty was that my womb was cursed, and I could not bear any children. Although one slipped through, I haven't been able to conceive a child since. So, you offer me your firstborn, and we offer you eternity."

As we chatted, Gethambe came rushing into my room carrying something that was wrapped in a blanket. He was upset and crying. "What is it?" I asked.

"Can you feed her? Lana is refusing to be a mother to our daughter. If she doesn't feed, she will die. We don't have bottles and formula here," he pleaded.

"I have never had a baby before; I only experienced a miscarriage," I explained. "My breasts don't produce milk."

"If you are willing to accept this child as your own, I can give you the power to provide for her," Lilith said.

"So, she would become my daughter and not Lana's?" I questioned.

"Yes," she answered, bowing her head to me.

I've always wanted a child, but I didn't think this was how I would become a mother. I had always thought that it would happen the traditional way.

After thinking about this poor little baby and the threat she was facing, I had immediately decided to become her mother. "Yes. I will love her as if I gave birth to her myself."

Lilith walked around to the front of me and knelt. She caressed my breasts before inserting one into her mouth, gently sucking on the nipple. She twirled her tongue passionately around the nipple, flickering it intermittently until milk began to leak slowly from it. Then she did the same to the other one until it too revealed milk.

Then Gethambe handed me his daughter, and I uncovered her face to see that she looked like a real wolf pup. But her baby blue eyes caught me off guard. I saw nothing but peace and tranquility in them.

"With her first feed, her body will become human, and she will be able to see. Like regular wolf pups, they are born blind. Pull her to you," Na'amah directed. "And give your daughter life."

I held her in one arm and pulled her up to my breast. She toyed with it for a few seconds before taking my nipple into her tiny mouth. Hungrily, she sucked the milk that poured from my breast, and slowly she began to transform into a human baby. Her skin darkened just a little, becoming a beautiful coffee color, but her eyes remained sapphire blue. When she finished on one side, I moved her to the other breast and allowed her to continue feeding.

"Does she have a name?" I asked, looking at my new bundle of joy.

"We can name her whatever you like," Gethambe stated.

"I like the name Serenity. I believe she will bring much of that to my life," I smiled, becoming smitten with my daughter.

"I like that," Gethambe said. "Serenity."

We all sat there and watched my daughter feed until she couldn't take any more milk from my breasts. It was a joyous occasion, something that I wished I could have done a long time ago. When I finished feeding her, Lilith took her and handed her to a chambermaid. She gave her orders to set up a bed in her room and tend to the baby while I went through the wedding ceremony. I had become attached to her so quickly and was ready to snuggle with her already. How could Lana be so cold to something so tiny and adorable?

"Now leave us, Gethambe, while we get your fiancé ready for your wedding," Lilith stated.

"Or allow us to play with that extremely large dick of yours," Na'amah giggled.

I could tell that he loved the flattery he was receiving from the elders, but he left happier than he had arrived.

Lilith and Na'amah continued to dress me and comb my hair, preparing me for the wedding. When they had finished, I knew everything that I was to do and everything that was to happen. When the moon was at its fullest, I was escorted into the ceremonial chamber with nothing but a sheer gown and veil. I couldn't wear their traditional color of white because I wasn't a virgin, so Lilith thought it would be fitting for me to wear an ivory gown sprinkled with gold glitter.

I was walked down the aisle by Pax and handed to Gethambe, who wore a robe similar to my gown. The elders lined one side of the room while Gethambe's loyal Canine Crew lined the other side.

The room was filled with purple candles that filled the room with a lavender fragrance. There were so many Star Gazer lilies that I could have gathered them up and made a queen size bed with them. The room was dim but set an erotic and romantic tone for the event that was happening.

The priest entered the room, bowed to Gethambe and then me. He then said a prayer to the Almighty as we held hands and gazed into each other's eyes. From the Holy Well of Elohim, he dipped the Golden Goblet of Life and filled it with the blessed water.

He handed the goblet to Gethambe first since he was the man, the protector, and the king. According to tradition, he drinks first, and the wife drinks second.

Looking at me, he drank from the cup and handed it back to the priest. He held the goblet into the air and said, "Protect this union, Lord Almighty, grant them a long life of happiness and bring Gethambe many sons. Let no man or beast break the bond that they will form tonight under the full moon with your blessing."

I looked at him and fell deep into his heart as he fell deep into mine. Everything about the marriage felt right, including the daughter that was given to me that I didn't bear. This made me wish I would have found this man earlier and become his first and only wife. But at least I have some part of him instead of none of him.

The priest then handed me the goblet, and I drank the sweet, blessed water. As I handed the goblet back to the priest, I felt a burning sensation in my chest, on my arm, and on my back. My body levitated from the floor, and I watched as my skin turned gold and lit the room with a dim, heavenly glow.

All the elders fell to their knees along with Samael, the parents, the Canine Crew, and my husband. I glanced over at the priest to find him too on his knees, thanking God for sending me to his people.

I watched as the etching of Aphrodite was drawn onto my stomach, giving me the power of reproduction, an etching of the Ankh was placed on my right shoulder that symbolized eternal life, down the middle of my back, the Gods etched the Djed symbol, which was the backbone of life, and then a cobra that swirled up my leg symbolizing power and royalty. Lastly, on the back of one hand was the Eye of Horus, granting me protection and good health, and on my palm of the other hand was the scarab, offering me the power of reincarnation.

"No woman in this pack has ever received so many gifts from the Gods in one day. It is normal for the men but highly uncommon for women," I heard Samael whisper to Lilith.

As my body slowly descended, I felt enlightened. I could hear everything, see glimpses of the future, and feel the slightest touch, sending waves of passion and love racing throughout my body. I was a new woman, an improved woman, a gift from the Gods to bring peace to all those around me.

I gave the goblet back to the priest who held it high into the air and yelled, "Praise the Almighty for showering this new queen with knowledge beyond our understanding. Bless this union between Gethambe and Ashley and let them flourish and reign as one ruler."

"I will love you from this day forth and into an eternal afterlife. You are the rhythm that makes my heartbeat with love. You are the sun that warms my blood. You are my beginning, and I am your ending. Ashley, I will lay down my life to spend forever with you," Gethambe stated.

"I will love and cherish your being. I will be submissive but supportive. I will listen to you and support your decisions. You are my king, my life, and my joy. I will give you many children and be a loving mother. Gethambe, I will give you the breath from my body so that you can breathe. Without you, there is no life in this world for me. I give all of me to you. Forever," I said my vows to him.

"Tonight, under the last full moon of the year, with the blessing of the Almighty and the support of the elders, I pronounce you man and wife. Now you must take your wife to her private chambers and consummate the marriage in front of your friends and family."

The priest tied a single white ribbon around our wrists, and we made our way to our chambers with the elders and his family close behind us. We entered the room first, stood at the foot of the bed, and waited for all who attended to join us.

When the door closed, Gethambe dropped to his knees and became intoxicated with my scent. He smelled my sweetness and licked it passionately through my gown.

I could feel as my cream began to trickle out, covering his tongue as he slurped it up. I removed my gown and opened my legs wide for him to taste all of me. Gethambe's tongue slid in and out of my sweetness as it flickered slowly across my clit.

I pulled his head in close as he grabbed my ass and dug his nails deep into it. Feeling his tongue pleasure my clit sent waves of ecstasy running through my body. I tilted my head backward and rode his tongue fervently.

I swirled my hips, I thrusted them forwards and backward, I allowed him to lick and suck my sweet juices as they spilled from their hiding place. I moaned as I pinched my nipples and pulled on them gently.

Gethambe stood up, and I looked into his crimson red eyes, then down to his long, thick dick, anticipating the moment that I would feel all of him inside of me. He grinned at me and licked his lips as he massaged his hardness.

I smiled deviously and then pushed him back onto the bed. His dick was hard and standing at attention, ready for me to take him into me. So, I climbed onto the bed and straddled him. Surprised, he looked at me, knowing that no woman has attempted to ride his dick since the Gods blessed him with his extraordinarily long and girthy steel rod.

I hovered over it for a few seconds while he held it in place, then slowly, inch by intimidating inch, I took him into me. Gethambe grabbed my ass and began to push and pull me in the direction he wanted me to go. I followed his lead as I leaned forward and steadied myself by placing my hands onto his chest.

I ground on him excitedly, bouncing a little with each swirl of my hips. I watched as his eyes rolled into the back of his head and listened as he growled with desire.

He felt so good inside of me as his massive hardness played blissfully with my g-spot. My body trembled with desire as it began to float in euphoria. I could feel my body warm; my heartbeat quickened as my clit thumped for a sweet release.

I could feel the excitement of Gethambe's hardness as it swelled inside of me and pulsated. He was pulling me down hard onto his rod as he thrusted up into my wetness. He was so deep into my cavern that I was unable to hold my climax back. I bounced as he thrusted up into me, making my body surrender all its secrets. My cream came rushing out of my body like a flash flood, covering his dick and balls.

Gethambe continued to push up into me, filling the room with loud slapping noises. His body was on fire, his nails extended, digging deep into my ass, but his beast was well controlled.

I could feel his pace quicken as his body shook uncontrollably. He howled as he released all his warm nectar into my core. His body bucked wildly, and I looked back and saw that his toes had curled under. He could barely breathe as spurt after spurt shot deep into me.

Lilith came running over to our bed and ran her hand across my stomach. She looked at me and said, "I grant you this pregnancy. These babies you will keep. Because you accepted a child that did not come from your womb and gave her life, I will leave your babies as a marital present from the elders. Congratulations."

"So, I'm already pregnant? You can tell that I'm already pregnant?" I asked, trying to catch my breath.

"Yes, my child. You are with children. Three to be exact," she announced, then Samael and his wives left the room.

"Nothing about tonight has been traditional. From

Lana giving up our daughter, to the priest who married us, down to the way you made love to me, and Lilith blessing us with the gift of our first pups, nothing about this has been traditional," he laughed.

As I tried to pull myself up, I was unable to move. "It will take about a half-hour for it to go down, and then you will be able to get up. Right now, he's too swollen to pull out of you without ripping you apart," Ebonee said, sitting on the bed beside us.

This all was a little new for me. I have never had anyone watch me have sex and then sit and hold a conversation with me while their son was still submerged deep into my wetness. To them, this was just another part of life. Nothing about sex was embarrassing to them.

"Your mother and I will be returning to Edom in the morning. Pax and Cherish will be accompanying us on the journey home. You need to try and fix that shit with Lana and help her to realize that she is a valuable member of this community before she does something that she will regret," my father warned.

"I will deal with her shenanigans after everyone has left. But as far as Serenity goes, Ashley is her mother. Lana will have no access to her. She will grow up knowing that I am her father, Ashley is her mother, and that she is a princess of survived death as it ran around her mothers' bed four times on the night of her birth," Gethambe told his father.

"I agree with that," my mother stated. "And welcome to the family, Ashley."

They left the room, and Gethambe finally was able to

pull out. He just wanted to hold me for the remainder of the night, and I was okay with that because I was tired.

I snuggled my body deep into his arms and fell swiftly to sleep.

I woke to a bag being placed over my head, my hand and feet being tied, and the faint cries of my daughter. I was confused and had no idea of what was happening to me. Although I tried to call out for Gethambe, I had no voice and no strength. But I heard a woman say, "Either give her to Bullet or take her and the baby out to the desert and bury their bodies. Don't just kill them; cause her just as much pain as she caused me."

I knew that couldn't have been anyone but Lana. But why was she now turning her back on me and wanting to cause me harm?

"Bullet will be in your debt for a long time," another voice said.

"Just keep her away from this pack. Take them and never return. Do it fast before Gethambe returns." she directed.

~To Be Continued~

MESSAGE TO THE READER

First, I would like to thank God for giving me the gift to write these stories. Without my faith in him, I would not flourish as an author or a person.

Secondly, I want to thank my husband and my family for their continued support because without their time, patience, and understanding – I wouldn't be able to give you my best. So, to the man that I love with all my heart, Terence Derone Smith, I appreciate all that you do. Your generosity has not gone unnoticed.

Finally, I thank you, the readers! As a new author, I appreciate your willingness to ride with me on this journey. You guys are just simply amazing!

I hope you enjoy this book as much as I enjoyed writing it. Please leave a review and tell me what you think and keep your eyes open for "Skinwalkers ∼ 2" because it's coming soon to Amazon!

ABOUT MONICA L. SMITH

Monica L. Smith lives a vast contrast in lifestyles. She has been working in the medical field since 1997, first as a Certified Nursing Assistant, then in 2005 as a Medication Aide, and, since 2013, as a Licensed Practical Nurse. She was born in Louisville, Kentucky, where she received her diploma. She then moved to Maricopa, Arizona, with her husband and 3 out of 9 children.

When she isn't working, she enjoys old-school television shows such as "Perry Mason," "Matlock," "Forensic Files," and more currently, "The First 48." Her creative side began to emerge when she tried her hand at writing. She published A Softer Side of Me, a book of 10 poems focusing on her "normal" but inspirational life, including her husband, children, and career. It spent time as #1 in the poetry genre on Amazon.

But much like her character, there's another side to Monica L. Smith, who has realized that she has a passion for urban erotic fiction. She enjoys writing what she calls "no-no" sensual sex scenes, and while she does explore the dark side, she also firmly believes in writing about finding love and hopes to inspire women to find their balance between sexuality and true love.

She claims she may not actually do what she writes about, but she feels a connection to it and enjoys the thrill that drives her to see her stories through to their exciting climax and conclusion.

KEEPING UP WITH MONICA

authoressmonicalsmith@gmail.com
https://www.authoressmonicalsmith.org/
https://twitter.com/AuthorMLSmith73
https://www.instagram.com/terrylynsmith/
https://www.facebook.com/authormonicasmith

Psst – Join my secret reading group
https://www.facebook.com/groups/readersthatwrite2
18+ Adults Only

ALSO BY MONICA L. SMITH